DEAD LAWYERS

A NOVEL

BY

NICK NOVICK

ISBN: 1-4033-4977-0 (e-book)
ISBN: 1-4033-4978-9 (Paperback)

This book is printed on acid free paper.

1stBooks – rev. 12/02/02

To Lila

I wish to thank the following organizations and persons for their time and information in the areas of their expertise. With the benefit of their patience and knowledge, this novel became a reality.

Los Angeles County Sheriff Department, Santa Catalina Island; Orange County Sheriff-Coroner Department; A1 Stop Non-Stop Training and Repair, Santa Ana, rebreathers; Len Miller, sailing enthusiast; Lisa Novick, author/editor, Richard Fukumoto, M.D., forensic expert.

All the above imparted their knowledge with clarity and depth. I am solely responsible for any errors made or variances taken in the name of literary license.

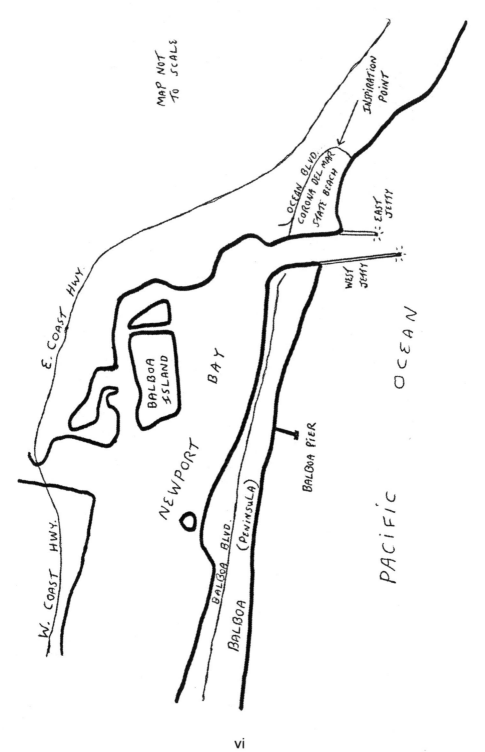

MAP NOT TO SCALE

INSPIRATION POINT

OCEAN BLVD.

CORONA DEL MAR STATE BEACH

EAST JETTY

WEST JETTY

E. COAST HWY.

W. COAST HWY.

BALBOA ISLAND

NEWPORT BAY

BALBOA PIER

BALBOA BLVD. (PENINSULA)

BALBOA

PACIFIC OCEAN

ONE

Careful, Jonathan thought, when he saw the police car in the next lane. A citation would postpone the killing. Heading south on Newport Boulevard in Costa Mesa, he flicked his eyes between the speedometer and traffic controls.

His final decision made sense. Alternatives weren't realistic. Gleefully hitting the steering wheel with his palm, he smiled, saluting fate, his fickle mistress.

Sharing his plan with someone who had similar convictions would validate his actions. Though they had never met, Rushton Fowler Jones always came to mind. There'd be no open encouragement from Rush. For the record he may even be antagonistic, but the goals would make them kindred spirits.

FRANCO POLPERRO swung his feet onto the cool hardwood floor, slipped off his pajama top, stepped out of the bottoms, put on a Speedo, and went to an undraped large window. His movements appeared choreographed.

"Hello." He picked up the telephone on the second ring.

"Hi, this is Ann. My apologies. I can't go swimming this morning. Monday is clear."

"Sorry. Monday then. Are we still on for tonight?"

"Definitely. See you then. Have a good swim."

He peered across Ocean Boulevard to the short, steep slope of Corona del Mar State Beach. With the large fee he had received yesterday, he'd be secure in owning this two-million-dollar Newport Beach home.

In his late thirties, he appeared older because of the artificially-enhanced gray in his straight, black, designer-cut hair. Exercise regimen kept his small physique looking athletic. Thin lips gave his wide mouth flexibility in showing anger, warmth, or whatever the occasion needed. Muscled shoulders emphasized a swimmer's waist.

Polperro stretched toward the ceiling and rotated the upper part of his body in a swimming motion. He'd have to hurry to keep his ten o'clock appointment.

1

OBJECTIVITY and making correct and timely decisions applies to any field of endeavor, Jonathan thought, even like the unusual one facing him this morning.

Thick blond hair roofed his rugged face. Blue eyes that bore the pain of shin splints, twisted ankles, heel spurs, aching knees and rotator cuff problems, were the road map of trying to make the body overcome middle-age. Below his left eye, a vertical two-inch military-combat scar stood out as a fixed barometer of physical endurance.

THROWING ON A TERRY ROBE and stepping into topsiders, Polperro grabbed swim goggles and ear plugs, went down the stairs and quietly exited to Ocean Boulevard. Looking at the gentle ocean swells and anticipating the exhilaration of a one-mile swim, he couldn't think of a better way to start a day.

ENTERING NEWPORT BEACH, Jonathan crossed the bridge over West Coast Highway. Newport Bay shimmered to his left. Newport Boulevard merged into Balboa Boulevard, putting him on Balboa peninsula, where he deposited a letter in a curbside mail box.

The peninsula hadn't changed much in decades. Except for scattered pockets of wealth on the bay and ocean sides, many old one and two story commercial and residential buildings held the eye in a sameness until a belt of expensive homes dominated the tip.

In summer, the manned main lot on the west side of Balboa pier remained open twenty-four hours a day. People who fished from the pier, rented a boat from Davey's Locker, or took a day trip to Santa Catalina Island, began filling the lot as early as four in the morning.

He drove to the second intersection past old Balboa Theater, turned right and made his way to metered-parking spaces at Balboa pier's east side, a less conspicuous location for his task.

After pushing quarters into a parking meter, Jonathan opened the car trunk. On schedule. Sixty minutes to sunrise.

POLPERRO SPENT six hours a week visiting disabled seniors and abused mothers and children. Giving his valuable time made him feel more involved than just contributing money.

Tonight, at the Costa Mesa Center for Abused Children, a pizza delivery would be timed for Ann's and his arrival. He'd tell stories and finish with a video of *The Sound of Music,* always feeling he had received more than he had given. It increased his admiration of Ann that she considered it a fun date.

Walking east on Ocean Boulevard to Inspiration Point, he descended the steep walkway, laid his robe and topsiders a safe distance from the tide, and inserted ear plugs. The beach faced south. To his left was Inspiration Point. To the right were parallel jetties into the ocean, protecting the mouth of Newport Bay and separating the tip of Balboa peninsula from the mainland Corona del Mar State Beach.

He moistened his goggles. Swimming beyond the breaking waves, he stayed within the beachgoers' designated area. Turning west toward the jetty he began his swim, a Monday, Wednesday and Friday ritual, as he thought of how he had to extend himself to keep up with Ann the few times she had joined him.

HARRY SHIFTED in his waking moments when he heard footsteps on Inspiration Point walkway. A sigh of relief hissed from his mouth when it didn't appear to be anyone who'd arrest or attack him. Huddling against the rocks in the dry sand, he watched the figure place his clothing on the beach. Waiting five minutes, he picked up the robe and topsiders, stuffed them into a plastic bag and made his way to Ocean Boulevard. The items were worth at least two bottles of wine, but he'd settle for one.

JONATHAN put on a hooded wet suit, gloves and a heavily-weighted belt with a flashlight and small blunt instrument attached. Goggles dangled from his neck.

3

He secured a rebreather to his back, with a tube going over each shoulder. Picking up a spear gun, spear and fins, he locked the trunk, put the keys in a security pocket and walked toward the Wedge at the west jetty.

Halfway there he slipped into his fins, turned the mouthpiece switch to open, inserted it, adjusted his goggles, and entered the water. He surfaced at the end of the west jetty and checked for boats. All clear.

Submerging, he swam across the narrow mouth of the bay to the east jetty, surfaced, and stopped before the swells became troublesome. No one on the jetty. No boats nearby. He jammed the gun and spear into rock crevices above the water's surface.

Looking toward Inspiration Point, he saw a swimmer three hundred feet away and coming towards him. He hoped Polperro had kept to his rigid schedule. This swimmer was going to die. There'd be no way to establish identity before he killed him. Too bad if it's the wrong person, but that's what makes Greek tragedies.

Diving, he went out twenty feet from the jetty toward the swimmer. Standing on the ocean floor in ten feet of water, he tried to maintain his position. Bubbles gushed at the surface from the swimmer's rhythmic movements.

Jonathan guessed the approximate place where Polperro would stop, turn, and tread water for a moment before resuming his swim. Positioned behind the swimmer, he crouched on the ocean floor, pushed up and fin-kicked.

Polperro moved his goggles to his forehead and looked at the brightening landscape. His mood reflected his happiness. Ann didn't appear to be coming to him on the rebound from Rush. He moved the goggles back in position and prepared to complete his first lap. Tonight, he'd ask her to marry him.

His body sensed an eerie sudden and unusual turbulence behind and below. He started to turn. Something broke the surface as he exhaled, with no time to hyperventilate. The shock and surprise of the assault compounded the force of the external pressure enveloping his chest. With the last breath rushing out of his lungs, he gasped "Oh my God! What…" His body flopped to the side and he felt the ocean close over his head. Water muffled his last words.

The instinct not to breathe was destroyed by the suddenness of the assault and the forced exhalation. He violently sucked, demanding oxygen. Water poured into his lungs. Convulsing and struggling to free himself from death's grip compounded the nightmare of sinking into oblivion. Movements were involuntary. His last thoughts were of Ann and if anyone would ever know what had happened to him.

They were on the surface less than a second. Jonathan made it one motion. Pinning the swimmer's arms to his body near the elbows, he locked his hands on the swimmer's chest. Using his own body as a pressure base, he forced the swimmer to exhale. Falling back under the water he relaxed the chest pressure, hoping the swimmer's natural instinct to breathe would finish the task.

Kicking to the ocean floor, he held the swimmer for ten minutes, even though a person drowns faster in salt water than fresh water. Gradually releasing his grip, he remained alert and hoped the swimmer hadn't suffered a laryngospasm.

Moving the swimmer's goggles to his neck, Jonathan shined a light on the face and sighed in relief. Polperro. *The gods are with me.* Using the blunt instrument, he forced a quarter to the gum line between Polperro's upper-front teeth, then removed it. Someday he might leave a plug nickel there. The thought made him laugh. Great symbolism. Zeus would be pleased. A parody on Greek mythology.

Pressure bruises on Polperro's arms and chest were of no concern. Decomposition and hungry ocean creatures should destroy any forensic evidence of murder.

He pulled the body underwater for two hundred yards beyond the end of the west jetty, and let go. Polperro's body settled to the bottom. With current ocean temperatures, the body would decompose, fill with gases, and float to the surface in three to four days.

Jonathan kicked underwater to his spear gun, navigated his way around the jetties, speared a halibut on the way, and surfaced within a hundred yards of Balboa pier. *I can't tell my family about the big one that didn't get away.* Reaching the beach, he took off his fins and moved the goggles to his forehead. Within an hour he'd be home. *My kids love halibut. I nearly forgot, Jeff wants me to shoot baskets before school.* He thought of Polperro. *It's great to be a god.*

ANN DISAPPOINTED HERSELF. She had stopped going to the gym and didn't feel like the person who had competed in five iron woman and ten lesser triathlon events. Canceling this morning's swim with Polperro made her realize how much she used work to forget Rush.

Their love affair was over, but her anger flared. *Why hadn't Rush just accepted responsibility and put the incident behind him?* She squeezed shut her eyes and shook her head, trying to fling away her thoughts.

Glancing at the clock, six a.m., she grabbed jeans, a sweat shirt and tennis shoes for tonight's date with Polperro.

THEY WALKED UP *behind him as he unlocked his car. Something cold and hard pressed against his head. Spinning around, the gun barrel bit into his forehead.* "No! No! Don't!" *he shouted.*

They laughed, eyes furtive .

Kicking out, arms flailing, sobbing, begging, "No! No! Don't!" Jonathan fell out of bed.

TWO

Frightened and distraught, unable to control her hand, she kept hitting the wrong buttons. On the fourth try, Michelle Tabbetts heard the 911 connection and screamed, "Hurry! Hurry! My baby's dying!"

A series of questions from the operator went unanswered, having no import to her emergency. "Robbie's dying - please - please!"

AT FIVE O'CLOCK Saturday morning, 911 dispatched a rescue vehicle, fire engine and police car. They made their way north on Flower Street toward Santiago Creek.

The Tabbetts lived in a wealthy area of older individually-designed homes in the residential heart of old Santa Ana. Though immigration and business growth had since made it an island in a Spanish-speaking community, it was still occupied by financially well-off seniors and young white professionals because of its central location and proximity to government offices.

Medical Technician Ost and police Lieutenant Mike Briden pulled their vehicles up to Tabbetts' one-story early-California style home. Ost shouted to his partner, "Get the equipment!" as Briden and he ran over the flagstone pavement. Briden saw a tall, slim, barefoot woman, appearing to be thirty-five, frantically waving them in.

"Michelle Tabbetts?" asked Briden.

Crying, trembling, appearing exhausted, disheveled, she wore no make-up except for the slight mascara staining her face. Dabbing with trembling hands at swollen, red eyes, she bolted into the house ahead of them. Medical technicians followed.

They went through the living room to a hallway at the west side of the house. Turning into the third room on the right, she started to speak, choked, and pointed to a crib in the back corner of the large bedroom. Briden noticed a man standing in apparent indifference at the opposite wall.

Briden's law-enforcement experiences hadn't numbed his feelings. Steeling his vision and mind while swallowing hard and often, he didn't vomit. In the crib, on his back and apparently dead, wearing only a diaper, was a child of less than two years who appeared to have suffered a club-like beating.

Effecting life-saving procedures, a medic kept muttering, "We can't keep his heart and breathing going."

Briden grimaced. It's murder, he thought, yet those people are going to tell us the child fell out of the crib thirty times in one night. He rapidly rolled his shoulders and shook his dangling arms.

Briden's eyes remained on the child until the gurney, with Michelle Tabbetts trailing, disappeared out the bedroom door. Wheezing through his crooked nose, he caught himself just as he rolled his shoulders and shook his dangling arms.

Motioning to an officer, he snapped, "Go with Mrs. Tabbetts. Make sure the doctors know she's there. They'll not want to waste valuable time on unnecessary tests and inaccurate diagnoses. Record everything she says."

Glancing around the room, he noted three walls of Robbie's bedroom were hand painted with a scene of the Serengeti plains. The fourth wall had artistic drawings of African musical instruments. A red Persian rug, with subdued blues, appeared to draw heat from the Serengeti. Wall lamps were appropriately placed. Tasteful and expensive decor dominated the room.

Introducing himself to Thomas Tabbetts, Briden was about to ask why he hadn't gone to the hospital with his wife and son. Tabbetts ignored the introduction and turned away.

Tabbetts' clean-shaven face set off his semi-baldness and gray hair. He appeared to be in his late fifties. Bare feet and legs protruding from the shorts appeared to have spent their life in sublime retreat under a desk. His nails looked professionally done. He picked at them with a file. What Briden could see of the body under the shirt was consistent with the picture he received. Totally cerebral. The welfare of the body entailed neatness and cleanliness, not healthful dieting and exercise.

Tabbetts didn't appear to be in sorrow or turmoil, as though Robbie's injuries demanded only an objective business-like decision.

"Mr. Tabbetts, Robbie appears to have been beaten, what happened?"

Tabbetts responded with a blank expression.

Briden, troubled by the callousness, controlled his impatience and held his usual faint smile. "What happened? It could save precious minutes in the medical team's work."

"I'm calling my lawyer. Please get out of my house." A well modulated and deep voice sounded as though giving orders and making decisions were routine. He held up an arm, pointing to the door.

Briden tightened his fists behind his back, relieving his anger. "No more questions."

Loudly replying, he again pointed to the door, "Good, now get out!"

"I'm sorry, we won't do that!"

Tabbetts sounded unaccustomed to having his orders disobeyed. "Get out!"

"We're legally here on an emergency, with reason to think a felony has been committed. I'm getting a telephonic search warrant."

"I'll sue!"

Controlling his anger, Briden couldn't comprehend Tabbetts' priorities. "The little boy is dying or dead!" His wiry-slim body cast off its slight slouch as he drew himself erect and brushed back his red hair. He wanted to release the pressure by rolling his shoulders and shaking his dangling arms, but Tabbetts might take it as a belligerent act. He made no effort to control his wheezing. His slight smile faded as he spoke in his James Cagney-like deliberate and lilting manner. Pointing to a police officer, Briden forcefully said, "Until our search is through, that officer is going to be with you every moment. Get used to it!"

IT WASN'T THE WAY Rush wanted to live, but he never thought his breakup with Ann would last six months. Though the small apartment in Tustin served his needs, nothing about it compared favorably to Ann's large Turtle Rock home. He'd been too busy with criminal trials to look for larger quarters.

The police had called him late Friday night about the possible death of Polperro. He wanted to call Ann, but feared it might come off as a way of trying to see her again.

He picked up a criminal file with a Monday trial date. Working without interruption at home on Saturdays was a plus in his profession. Joe Broxton would arrive in three hours.

A SOFT, SHORT knock on the door prompted Rush to push his shirt into his Levis and walk shoeless to the door. Opening it, a huge man filled the frame. "Rushton Fowler Jones? I'm Joe Broxton, private investigator."

Rush feared his fingers would be crushed as Broxton's hand wrapped around his like butcher paper holding a single pork chop. Pressure was light but firm. Broxton might be concerned about his intimidating physical image. Pointing to the living room, Rush took a seat on the sofa as Broxton settled into a large armchair.

The investigator's soft-spoken manner also belied his size. "What is it you'd like me to do?"

Rush wanted to keep his bitter memories buried and hoped Broxton would leave. Yet, he had to face a past that had misshaped an area of his personality and driven Ann away.

Since sixteen he had been on his own, putting himself through undergraduate and law school and had been recognized as the outstanding criminal prosecutor in California in 1998. He had fought learning about his background because he had won the battle to adulthood on his own.

Maybe he'd never be back with Ann, but perhaps he'd be a better person for the next woman in his life if he got some answers. Swallowing hard to loosen the constriction of his throat, he replied, "I want to find my mother and father."

"When and where did you last see them?" Broxton took a notebook and pen from a coat pocket.

"I've never seen them." Words came uneasily.

Broxton raised his head as he stopped writing. "Have you ever heard from them, been in contact with them?"

He shook his head. "Never. I don't know who they are, if they're alive, if I'm an illegitimate child, nothing." Saying it made him feel the vast empty space in his life.

"Is Rushton Fowler Jones your birth name?"

"Someone left me, weeks old, on an orphanage doorstep in Colorado. The name was on a piece of paper pinned to my blanket."

"Birth date on the note?"

"No. The orphanage gave me a birth date."

"Whoever left you there probably wanted you to have your true name. They didn't want to be traced so it's a safe bet you have no other connection to Colorado."

"That makes it difficult."

"Yes, but we have a couple of strong points in our favor."

"Like what?"

"The information world has drastically changed in the thirty-some years since you were born. And, though finding parents named Jones could be a nightmare, Rushton Fowler adds an interesting element. We'll know more after a little research." Broxton paused, as if wanting Rush to read his mind and be prepared for what he was going to say. "You have an important decision to make."

"I know."

"When I find them, if they're still alive, who makes the personal contact, and how? You won't be solving anything unless you have a specific purpose and goal."

"I want to meet them, but I'm scared and angry. They abandoned me, yet I want to know them. I'm not sure I can handle it if they don't want to see me." Hesitantly, he added, "It could make matters worse. Perhaps I should leave things as they are. It's a known quantity I've lived with."

"You need answers." Broxton tried to shift his weight in the armchair. It moved with him so he gave up. "You've never before tried to find them?"

"No." He felt guilty saying it and was compelled to add, "Nor have they tried to find me."

"Why haven't you tried? You're successful, you have resources."

11

Nick Novick

Rush spoke methodically. "My parents abandoned me so why should I wonder why? I have a life to live. Some foster homes are not a pleasant experience. Barbs from kids added to my resentment. Yet, between my youth and today I had to live with not a single day passing when I didn't think about them and how different, better, my life might have been if I could have shared it with family."

Saying it shattered the isolation of the hurt. Rush clenched his teeth and squeezed his moist eyes. Would Ann and he still be together if he had done this five years ago?

Broxton struggled out of the armchair by placing his hands on the arms and catapulting himself. "It happens all the time. Luckily the pros had benches on the sidelines."

Rush laughed and saw him to the door.

"I'll keep in touch."

THREE

Promotions didn't entail a larger office. Rush still had space for only two visitors' chairs and the view from the window was increasingly blocked by files stacked on the bookcase. Gray-metallic furniture added to the cold and uncomfortable look, reflecting the severity of the courthouse. Prosecutors were the only difference from one office to the next.

Standing and stretching, he felt old. Because he hadn't been in a triathlon for eight months, his gut was expanding proportionately. He took a large cloth envelope from the top drawer of his desk and removed a framed photograph. After they broke up, Ann had asked him not to display it.

Yours Forever,
Ann

Childhood scars made him unable to admit mistakes in his personal life. All survivors have scars.

Making an audible growl, he tried to clear his head. Filing through mail, he saw a letter without a return address, bearing a Newport Beach postmark of the day Polperro had disappeared. It raised interest and suspicion. Putting on latex gloves and holding it by the edges, he slid a letter opener under the flap. It contained a single sheet of writing paper. A typewritten quotation held the center of the sheet.

There is no evil without its compensation.
Seneca. Epistulae ad Lucillium

In the legal sense, he hoped the quotation was true. In a broader sense, he wondered why it had been sent to him and the purpose of it. He placed the anonymous letter in a plastic bag and filed it under *Miscellaneous-Open*.

SERGEANT BILL SULLIVAN, Orange County Sheriff-Coroner's Office, sat in his harbor patrol office on Newport Bay. He picked up the telephone, listened intently and hung up.

"Order the patrol boat to secure the area at the mouth of the bay. Start the fire-patrol boat!" The two-man fire-patrol boat had a working platform for picking up a body. Polperro had disappeared three days ago.

Nathaniel Benedict, a prominent Newport Beach investment manager who had bilked Sullivan's in-laws and other wealthy investors out of a large portion of their personal wealth, had been defended by Polperro. Benedict lived on Lido Isle in the requisite large home, drove a Rolls, and had all the other appearances of success. He had met most of his clients on the social circuit, eventually accepting their offers to let him manage their investments. Losses were over sixty million. Benedict had transferred title to everything he owned, and to most of the investment money, to his wife, hiding it through multiple transfers between off-shore banks.

Arriving at the scene, Sullivan noted it was a human body, not a life-sized doll dumped overboard from some raucous yacht party. With the body on board, Sullivan took his first long look. Ocean creatures had eaten the greater portion of the eyeballs, nose, ears, lips and genitals, along with other pieces of flesh. Except for the blue sapphire ring on the little finger of the left hand, he couldn't identify the body as Polperro.

JONATHAN LEANED BACK in his executive chair and closed his eyes. He thought of how defense attorney Polperro, wearing a three-piece navy-blue truth suit, had defended Nathaniel Benedict on multiple criminal fraud charges. Polperro repeatedly reminded the jury Benedict had a constitutional right not to take the stand, but that he testified because he wanted to be honest and lay himself open to prosecutor's questions. Polperro did not admit Benedict would use the same con-artist personality with the jurors that had enabled him to bilk trusting investors.

"Ladies and Gentlemen of the jury," Polperro had pontificated, "Mr. Nathaniel Benedict may have been negligent, sloppy, stupid, and used poor judgment in his investment business. But those acts aren't criminal." The crux of his argument was that "Benedict never did any act to *intentionally* defraud the investors of their money. *Intent to defraud* is necessary to make it a crime.

"If he has committed civil wrongs in trying to help his investors prosper, that is for a civil trial, another court, another jury."

Not-guilty. Years from now the investors might get a favorable verdict on their civil lawsuit. Appeals would grind on forever as they tried to find the money and get control of it. Benedict would continue to make the social circuits in Newport Beach, finding others still willing to invest with him. Greed and stupidity are not the province of the poor.

SULLIVAN DIALED his father-in-law. "Good morning, Mark. I think we recovered Polperro's body."

A pause and sigh appeared to show a feeling of sadness tinged with satisfaction. "Thanks."

Some of the victims had met at Mark's house on the evening of the verdict, making statements influenced by alcoholic beverages. Sullivan didn't want to remember. If the facts came out, his then silence would now be defenseless.

Bilked investors didn't like their first personal experience with the criminal system. Nor did they want to admit there was no difference between what their civil attorneys had done for them to keep their victims off their backs, versus what Polperro had done for Benedict.

One investor angrily said, "Kill that scum Benedict!"

Another shouted, "No. Kill the lawyers. Kill Polperro!"

No voice of reason, dissent or restraint countered those comments. No one laughed. Everyone looked in different directions, hiding their conspiratorial thoughts. If Sullivan had offered a plan for action, he felt agreement and funds would have been immediate.

WITH A LIGHT TOUCH of mascara, and dressed in a black pant suit, Michelle Tabbetts walked uneasily into Briden's office. Though she felt tense, a good night's sleep, fortified by tranquilizers, had blunted the sharp edges of fatigue and sadness.

On the back wall were photographs of uniformed men and commendations. Another wall held Police Olympics and firearm marksmanship trophies.

A newer dark-green carpeting covered the floor, in stark contrast with the hospital-white walls. Cottage cheese ceilings reflected the building's age and that renovations and refurbishing were budgeted piecemeal. In ten years, if the improvements lasted, they might come together and look like someone had a plan.

Briden rose and invited her to sit on the sofa. Michelle chose a chair close to his desk.

"Are you ready for this meeting?"

Michelle clenched her hands and nodded. She opened her handbag and took out a cigarette and lighter.

Briden quietly asserted his authority. It'd favor him for the remainder of their talk. "Please, no smoking."

Anger appeared to flare in her face, resenting his command, but she returned the items to her handbag.

"Shall we proceed?"

"Go ahead." Her face stiffened, as if to fortify herself.

He looked for other emotions or changes in expression. There were none. She was obviously still in shock. There was no other way to decipher her not breaking down. Hopefully, she wouldn't also have a nicotine fit.

Briden took a slow deep breath, turned on the tape recorder, and filled in the necessary details along with her Miranda rights. Much to his surprise, she didn't ask for a lawyer. He didn't know whether her answers would make her friend or foe. "Does your live-in help, Carmen Gonzales, have relatives locally?"

"No."

"Last time you saw her?" Briden sped up the tempo to see how quick and specific the answers came.

"About 5 or 6 Friday evening. The night before I found Robbie and called 911."

"Had she gone somewhere?"

"Carmen wanted the night off - a personal matter." She continued to sit erect. Her hands were still even though Briden felt she was craving a cigarette.

With short, quick questions, her answers were immediate. No one, thought Briden, could come in and lie with such ease and readiness under these circumstances.

"Do you know where she went?"

"No."

"What's her background?"

"She was a live-in with a neighbor's family for ten years. We employed her eight years ago when that family moved out of state." She didn't take her eyes from Briden's.

"When was she supposed to return from her night off?"

"By eight the next morning, the morning of Robbie's death."

"Did she?"

"Not that I'm aware of."

Briden lightly bounced the pencil eraser on his desk top. "Was that unusual?"

"She had never before failed to keep to her schedule."

"Has she ever struck Robbie in any way?"

"Never!" She stood and slowly paced six steps back and forth. "Don't mind me, I need a cigarette."

Briden ignored the implied request to smoke. "How do you know she didn't come back during the night, beat Robbie and leave?"

Michelle's stopped pacing. Her eyes widened, as though she had never considered that. "No! She wouldn't do that!"

"Do you think a jury would ignore all the evidence about Carmen's opportunity to commit the crime and her unexplained disappearance?"

"I guess not."

"Do you have any explanation as to why the first time Carmen fails to return on schedule is the day on which Robbie is murdered and she's made no attempt to contact you and explain her absence?"

Michelle shrugged. "She's an illegal, probably afraid."

He flipped through the file as he thought about her demeanor. He had detected no hesitation, no desire to blame a person who had disappeared, and no half-answers. Briden leaned back in his chair, intending to let her feel she wasn't being intimidated. The questioning would now be slow and deliberate.

"Do you know who killed Robbie?" Test her loyalties.

She returned to her chair. "My husband, Thomas." Her body went limp and she put her hands to her face, without crying. It appeared more a moment of agony than sorrow.

Briden recovered from the directness of her reply. "Proof?"

Michelle spoke through her hands. "Carmen left on Friday night. I got Robbie ready for bed. He had a few bruises at that time but was alert and playful. Thomas was the only person home with Robbie after I left the house."

"Where were you?"

She took her hands from her face and sat erect. "Charity work."

He stood so he'd have a more commanding figure for any accusation. "What time did you get home?"

"About four-thirty in the morning, a half-hour or so before I called 911."

Briden raised his eyebrows, knowing that answer wouldn't sit well with a jury. "What did you do during that interval?"

"I fixed a nightcap, sat in a chair and tried to find something on TV. Just before going to bed I checked on Robbie and found him in that condition. I was confused and frightened, awakened my husband, and called 911."

"If your husband and you were the only ones home with Robbie why shouldn't I believe that you - or both of you - had beaten him and then called the police, that your husband's silence is his way of protecting both of you, and now you plan to throw the blame on him?"

Michelle bowed her head as tears fought their way free from an attempt to look strong. Briden handed her a box of tissues. Her head came up. "Robbie was my son. I could never harm him or allow anyone else to do so."

"He was also your husband's son, wouldn't he feel the same?"

Michelle held his gaze. "Robbie was not my husband's son."

For the moment, Briden ignored the implications of that answer as related to Michelle's being a prosecution witness. The paternity issue might be reason enough for Michelle or her husband to want Robbie dead. "Does your husband know that?"

The reply held guilt and anxiety. "No."

FOUR

"I don't know how Polperro could've drowned unless he had suffered a stroke or been struck by something." Rush mentioned some of the possible forensic details of an autopsy.

"Who cares. He's dead. The city is cleaner without Polperro, but for three days he polluted the ocean." Briden shifted his slouched position as Rush cleared files from his desk.

"You don't feel sorry or perturbed by his death?"

Drawing a deep breath, Briden straightened, wheezed, and planted both feet on the floor. "When people like Polperro die, I don't feel society has lost a Mother Teresa and I don't feel any less a person because I don't mourn him. I didn't wish him dead and I wouldn't kill him. Now that he's dead, I feel no pain."

"I admire your honesty and disagree with your viewpoint." Rush stood and walked back and forth in the limited space behind his desk.

"Deep down I'm sure you feel the same way, Rush. You and I, witnesses and victims, have suffered the unethical practices of some criminal defense attorneys."

Rush opened a file. "It's inherent in the system."

"Come on Rush, it's more than that. Remember when the church warden's daughter was kidnaped, raped and murdered, the defense waited until the last day of your evidence and then claimed..."

Rush nodded and waved his hand. "Let's drop it. The criminal justice system is far from perfect. We both agree that if Polperro was murdered his killer should be found and brought to justice. Now, tell me about the Tabbetts' case."

"The suspects are Michelle Tabbetts and or Thomas Tabbetts and or Carmen Gonzales. Michelle Tabbetts states her husband did it. Carmen Gonzalez has disappeared. Thomas Tabbetts isn't talking." He made a full report.

Rush nodded. The death of a physically-abused child raises an inherent problem. The police just can't arrest everyone in the household and charge them. It's necessary to prove a particular person inflicted the injuries, subject to accomplices, conspiracies and other legal theories.

Briden absentmindedly looked at his hands. "The father is the owner of a large stock brokerage house. Impeccable record and character, socially prominent and well-liked in the community." Briden appeared as though he were going to say more, but stopped.

Rush noticed. "So? And?"

"Ann is his attorney."

He smiled wearily. "His money and Ann's abilities." He didn't add her middle initial *C.* Using it had entailed some of the worst moments in their relationship.

Rush held up the anonymous letter and explained his receipt of it.

> *There is no evil without its compensation.*
> *Seneca. Epistulae ad Lucillium*

"I relate this quotation to a significant felony around the date of the postmark. I'm excluding the common and expected dope, gang, skid-row murders and the like."

Briden replied, "The Tabbetts' boy or Polperro?"

"Polperro."

"Why not Tabbetts?"

"The *evil*, the three suspects in the Robbie Tabbetts' murder, haven't been *compensated*, that is, killed or harmed. Polperro's been *compensated* because of his *evil* acquittal on the Benedict case."

"What's the postmark on the letter?"

"Newport Beach, Friday, the day Polperro disappeared."

Briden pushed a new direction. "Assuming Polperro's autopsy indicates an accidental drowning, why would a killer want to tell us it was murder?"

"Let's pursue that. Is the letter writer an innocent person making an observation about crime in general?"

"Probably not. There'd be no reason to be anonymous," Briden reflected.

21

Rush shrugged and drummed his fingers on the desk. "The real question is, why would the sender want us to know Polperro was murdered - if he was murdered? Does he think I'd like what he's doing? He wants my approval, wants to know someone is with him in spirit?"

Briden nodded. "And on what he's going to do?"

Rush frowned. "If Polperro's a homicide and the killer intended to end it there, the letter serves little purpose. I suspect we may have a serial killer and we're in on the ground floor."

THE MAVERICK SEVEN-STORY Santa Ana office building was either an eyesore or an imaginative architectural triumph. No reflecting-glass panels or conforming colors of blues or greens went into its design. Michelle Tabbetts described it as twenty-first century Orange County bordello.

Tabbetts had started his business before parts of Santa Ana became a gang-shooting war zone. He felt tied to the location. Ten years ago he built an above-ground garage at the rear of the building with direct access to each floor of offices.

She felt a strong sense of pride. Thomas Tabbetts had arrived in Orange County in the seventies and pioneered low-cost brokerage fees, with professional advice, when the field was dominated by high costs and subtle churning of portfolios. It became the largest privately-owned stock brokerage on the west coast. Michelle became the trophy wife.

Entering her husband's office, she sat on a sofa on the far side of the room. She took out a cigarette, lit and snuffed it. Briden's admonition still lingered. Finishing his telephone call, he turned to face her.

She spoke as if by rote. "All that talk about a large family was just talk, wasn't it? Robbie's existence interfered with your freedom and mobility." She stopped, deciding he wasn't listening.

He dug under a fingernail with a file, as though one speck of dirt would spoil his image.

"Why didn't you say you didn't want children? Don't you realize how it affected our marriage? And now this?"

Silence.

"I've arranged a memorial service for Thursday afternoon." Michelle didn't want her frustrations to show her anger. But, unable to contain her exasperation, she said, "For God's sake, Squeaky Clean, would you for once put away that nail file, it's like an appendage!"

In a calm and measured voice, he said, "Life goes on." He looked at his reflection in the large window behind him. "You have to be able to take your losses. It's like a stock transaction."

She jumped up, shaking, shouting, "How can you say that?"

Tabbetts stood and didn't reply as he ran his tongue over his front teeth as if to clean them.

Michelle sat and sobbed uncontrollably. "He's dead! Robbie's dead! Don't you care?"

No reply.

"I was questioned by the police."

"And you told them I killed the kid?"

Michelle screamed, jumping up again, "Robbie! Robbie!" and then waited until she had better control. "His name was Robbie. Just like shares of stock carry a name," mockingly adding, "Like GE, IBM, AT&T."

He sat, repeating his question. "You told them I killed the kid?"

Her reply had a raw edge of emotion and fact. "Yes, can you convince me otherwise?"

"What about Carmen Gonzales?"

"Is that the road your attorney is taking?"

"There are two roads." He held up two spread fingers, then brought them together.

"Just like the stock market, diversify to cut your losses." Bitterly, she added, "Carmen Gonzales or me or both of us, as long as it isn't you."

Coldly, he replied, "He was fine when I went to bed. How do I know you didn't do it?"

"Me? I loved him. He's my son. Why would I kill him?"

"You were afraid I'd divorce you. Getting rid of the kid would put everything right."

Her voice quivered as she stood and faced him. "What do you mean, divorce, what have I done?"

"Michelle, if I fall you go down with me. The kid was not my son."

She stumbled to the sofa. His statement pierced the last veil of respect they had between them. "How? What? Where did you get..."

"Do you think you could do the party circuits and not get opportunities to be involved with other men? That I don't have any friends? I ran the kid's DNA. No match."

"Do you have anything else to say?"

His voice sounded conciliatory. "Michelle, whatever happened to us?"

"It doesn't matter anymore. Robbie's death makes it irretrievable, and one of us is going to be convicted of murder."

DR. BEN MET RUSH at the entrance to the Sheriff-Coroner's building on Santa Ana Boulevard, Santa Ana. They shook hands and went to an office off the front hallway.

Dr. Ben Stabinsky's parents had emigrated from Scotland to California after World War II. He was born in 1948 in rural south Orange County and eventually completed University of California, Los Angeles, medical school. The gangland jungles of Los Angeles, where he'd experience the forensics of gunshot and knife wounds, drug deaths and other criminal-act autopsies, attracted him.

Dr. Ben's forensic conclusions were recognized as impartial. He gathered evidence as a specialist and presented it to a jury like a layman. His thorough explanations prevented a criminal defense attorney from playing mind games.

Tall, bulky and in reasonably good physical shape, he ran five miles every morning. Strong Slavic features gave him a commanding countenance.

Ten years ago he joined the Orange County Sheriff-Coroner's Office and advanced to become Chief Coroner.

Newport Beach police, the harbor patrol, and Rush had given Dr. Ben information on Polperro.

Dr. Ben settled in a chair. "The cause of death was drowning, but how do we prove the manner of death - a battery, for example - caused the drowning, making it murder?"

"Let's go through the death categories: natural, accident, murder, suicide or undetermined."

"I'd call it murder, but that's by a process of elimination and it would never hold up in court. Polperro was financially successful. There were no signs of a natural death. I saw no indication of any illness that might have caused him to commit suicide. No heart attack. No trauma, no underlying tissue damage from being hit by a boat or jet ski or being smashed against the jetty. I'm not a psychiatrist, but this man had the world by the tail. We took tissue samplings for drug testing and I expect that to be negative."

"So, drowning was the cause of death."

Dr. Ben stood, paced, and nodded. "Frothiness in the glottis and air passages, though it's a strong indication of drowning, was minimal due to putrefaction. His lungs were filled with water, and that, subject to other evidence, is an indication of drowning. As you know, if a dead person is thrown into the water, we don't expect to find water in the lungs." Dr. Ben stopped pacing and sat down.

"Go on." Rush changed his sitting position.

"The sooner the body is recovered, the better the evidence in determining whether it was a drowning. When putrefaction takes hold, the water in the air passages will have shifted, the lungs rot with gases and the chemistry of the blood is disturbed."

"What about congestion and cyanosis in the right side of the heart? Were the principal veins distended with dark blood, giving medical indications of a drowning?" asked Rush.

"Due to time in the water, decomposition, there was minimal evidence of that condition to support a drowning."

"What about diatomaceous matter?"

Dr. Ben reflected, "We found circulated diatoms in intact tissues and that may be the best specific evidence indicating drowning. We also found diatomaceous matter in the stomach, which showed the fluid there wasn't from pulmonary edema or simple drinks. But what caused him to drown?"

"If someone drowned him, it was accomplished with minimal physical force and no struggle."

"Correct," replied Dr. Ben.   "But doesn't that seem impossible to do?   Polperro was small but physically conditioned. Without using some blunt force to incapacitate him, how do you drown a good swimmer?"

"Let's agree there's no blunt-force trauma. If Polperro fought off an attacker, wouldn't the exertion cause the eyeballs to bleed - petechial hemorrhaging."

"Body decay," Dr. Ben shook his head as an apparent completion of the sentence, "besides, ocean creatures ate most of the eyeballs."

"Anything else?" Rush asked.

"Yes, he didn't suffer laryngospasm from the shock of being attacked or the breathing in of water. That's when the muscles contract around the larynx, the throat closes or collapses, and the person suffocates because he can't breathe.   That'd normally mean no water in the lungs. And, he would've come to the surface sooner."

"What if someone surprised him so quickly and forcefully he had no opportunity to fight back?" Rush stood and stretched, hoping to exert more life into his thinking. "He'd probably receive bruises on his body wherever he was held. Would putrefaction and ocean creatures do away with that evidence?"

"If that did happen, the underlying tissue would nevertheless show bleeding if Polperro received bruises while he was still alive." Dr. Ben slouched. "That's the one piece of evidence I have. How would an attacker minimize a struggle?"

"By pinning Polperro's arms to his side, from behind, and pulling him under the water. But, could another swimmer do that? Think about the circumstances. A murderer would have to be equipped for diving and probably heavily weighted, waiting under the water. Besides, wouldn't the diver's bubbles give him away?"

Dr. Ben nodded. "I agree. Well, I examined the underlying tissue in the areas around the elbows. Those tissues showed evidence of bleeding from bruises or abrasions."

"If he had been dead when those tissues were damaged, the heart wouldn't be pumping blood and the tissues wouldn't show bleeding. Nor could it come from a dead body being knocked around on the bottom of the ocean by the currents."

Dr. Ben nodded and sat upright. "A major point to support our attack theory is that the location of the bleeding tissues on both arms is almost identical."

Rush's smile changed to a frown as he furiously drummed his fingers on the table.

"What's wrong?"

"I just thought of the front-page photo in the Los Angeles Times when the jury acquitted Benedict."

"So?"

"Benedict is a large man. He was so happy with the acquittal he gripped Polperro in the area of the elbows and lifted him out of his chair as if he were a rag doll. That was two days before Polperro's death. It's arguable that caused the tissue damage."

Dr. Ben agreed. "So we're forced to think ass-backwards. That is, we don't believe it was suicide, undetermined, natural or accidental, so it has to be murder. No judge or jury will buy that, we need to prove the manner of death indicating murder."

Rush drummed his fingers. He was losing his consciousness that the habit might annoy people. If some people furiously chewed gum or said ten *you know's* in every sentence or gesticulated with every word, why in the hell couldn't he drum his fingers? He had picked up the habit from his mentor in Beach County before applying for a position with the Orange County D.A.'s office. "It's the little things that keep coming up telling me this is more than an accidental drowning. But, little things aren't enough."

Dr. Ben raised his eyebrows. "Like what. Something you haven't told me?"

"Part of it's in the reports. Polperro's goggles were around his neck when the body came to the surface. If for some reason I stop while I'm swimming, I move my goggles to my forehead. That way, the head band is still in place and it's easier to put them back on. I had Newport Beach police talk to Ann and she said Polperro would stop near the jetty, turn around, push his goggles to his forehead, tread water, and look at the sunrise landscape. I assume Polperro did that routine the day he drowned. If he did, stopping and treading water would make it easier to attack him from behind, as opposed to attacking a swimmer in motion. And, whether they were over his eyes or on his forehead, the goggles couldn't possibly have come down to his neck. If anything, they would have come off his head and now be somewhere in the ocean."

Neither spoke, contemplating, as if waiting for a revelation. Nothing more needed to be discussed at this point. They shook hands and parted. Rush believed Polperro's death was the first of a series of murders, but he didn't know if the targets would include criminals. The war on crime would never be resolved, it's only the trials, the battles, that give the appearance of finality. Even there, victims were never victorious.

If Polperro had been murdered, why would the killer send the letter to me? Rush's excellent conviction record had given someone the wrong impression. This case could ruin his career. That Polperro had been Ann's new boyfriend makes the situation even more difficult.

The killer has chosen me as his confidant.

JESSICA SAT on the sofa and held Jonathan's hands. "Did you read the letter from the District Attorney's office?"

"No."

She hesitated, wanting him to control his reaction to the letter. "Are you going to Texas?"

He shook his head. "I don't know. How many times have I been there and…" He shuddered. "I feel helpless. The system is helpless."

Jessica hugged him. "We'll get through this." A soft kiss on his cheek. "We'll get through this."

FIVE

SAM HORNE liked the unplanned sexual encounter. It heightened desire. Naked, on his stomach, he enjoyed the rhythmic pressure traveling up and down his spine. "Oh-h-h-h, that feels good. Massage the shoulders, too."

The kneading reached his shoulders, sometimes straying to his neck muscles. "Are you relaxing?"

Horne sighed. "It's a wonderful appetizer. I can't wait to make love."

Starting to roll over, a gentle force pushed him back to his stomach. "A few more minutes. We have forever."

That intrigued Horne. "Forever? I wish it could be that way with every lover. Isn't it unsettling to know we'll probably never see each other again?"

"I live the moment of love. If it lasts, good. If it doesn't, I have the memory."

"I understand."

"I'll loosen your neck muscles."

Horne felt pressure on his neck. Blood filled his head. "I don't...what's happen..." A feeling of weightlessness. Darkness.

Pressure had been applied to the carotid arteries for seconds. Quickly putting on latex gloves, Jonathan grabbed Horne's belt, passed the end through the buckle and placed the loop around his neck with the buckle at the side. Again, he briefly applied finger pressure to the carotid arteries. *Horne must be alive when I strangle him.* Lying prone on Horne's back, he cinched the belt above the Adam's Apple with enough pressure to strangle him. Jonathan's weight, the belt cinching, and Horne's unconsciousness, held Horne's body spasms to a minimum. Horne's aborted movements didn't cause the belt to move about the neck any more than it would have had he hanged himself.

With one knee on the floor against the bathroom door, Jonathan supported the upper part of Horne's body, face down, across his other thigh. He knotted the end of the belt to the doorknob and held the body as he pulled back, lowering Horne's body until the belt, with the buckle at the side of the neck, became taut, leaving Horne's upper body slightly off the floor. Horne's free weight pulled the belt tighter. *Zeus should be pleased. Charon will be busy.*

Jonathan dressed, forced a quarter between Horne's upper two-front teeth and removed it. He wiped clean the few things he had touched. Checking the hotel hallway for passers-by, he placed the *Do Not Disturb* sign on the outside, and quietly stepped to the stairwell on the fifth floor.

Looking at his wristwatch, he said, "Great! I can still make it to The Bar. The gods are with me. Maybe I'll get even more lucky."

"COME ON, socializing will help you get a judgeship."

Rush didn't want to be associated with The Bar group. If he needed their support he'd have to be manipulative and hungry for power. "Thanks again but I've got much to do."

The Bar was a typical lunch and dinner restaurant-bar with its chief asset being the proximity of the alcoholic beverages to the county courthouse.

Rush thought of how the behavior of a few people adversely affected the criminal justice system. A few judges, politically-correct criminal prosecutors and defense attorneys, made up a large portion of the night crowd at The Bar. Prosecutorial careers were sidetracked or destroyed, and cases compromised, because of comments made in the eighty-six proof atmosphere. More than a few prosecutors feared the next late-morning entry into their offices by a bleary-eyed, hung-over supervisor who'd proceed to tell them, based solely on what the defense attorney or a judge had said, how they were mishandling a case.

FOUR CRIMINAL DEFENSE ATTORNEYS sat at a corner table in The Bar. Jonathan, wearing a baseball cap, eyeglasses, a fake moustache, and with his scar cosmetically covered, sat two tables away. Unless the attorneys raised their voices, he wouldn't be able to hear their conversation. He recognized only two of them. Kurt Baumholtzer was currently in trial defending an eighteen-year old for the robbery-murder of a 7-11 clerk. Stephen Maldive had been a prominent criminal defense attorney and recently announced he'd be retiring within the year. Jonathan didn't recognize the other two.

"I have," related Baumholtzer, "a handsome kid whose in-court demeanor appeals to the jury. His clean-cut family is quietly weeping in the front row every day. And, I have the SODDI defense - Some Other Dude Did It."

Two of the other attorneys laughed. *Defending Suspects 101* listed SODDI as an effective defense where the facts were applicable.

Appearing to be making notes from his reading material, Jonathan noted Baumholtzer was lefthanded. Every time he took a drink he adjusted his napkin's edge parallel with the edge of the table and set his glass in the center of the napkin, often adjusting it three times. He also moved the basket of pretzels to the center of the table when its location had been changed.

"So," asked Stephen Maldive, the attorney who didn't laugh at the SODDI defense remark, "do you think you'll get an acquittal? No, wait, that's the wrong question. Did the kid murder the clerk?"

"I'll be very surprised if I don't get an acquittal."

"But the kid was one of the murderers, right?" Maldive appeared perturbed and persisted in trying to get his question answered.

Baumholtz shrugged, not really wanting to delve into the issue any further. "Maybe. I don't know. That's what makes it so challenging." He paused, looked deeply at Maldive and asked, "What's your problem? Come on," he said as he gently slapped him on the back, "you know how the system works, you've had more big acquittals than any of us."

Maldive appeared morose. "Doesn't that make you sick inside? Don't you think it's wrong what we're doing?"

"Hey, I didn't see the kid do the murder and I didn't ask him if he did it. That leaves me clean. I use the system to beat the system."

Maldive vigorously shook his head. "We're perverts." Glassy-eyed, he looked at each attorney and appeared to have to force the words out of his mouth. "About three years ago I got so depressed I contemplated suicide."

Baumholtzer's voice became loud and filled with surprise and advice. "Suicide! Balls, Maldive, you gotta have balls."

"It's ethics, not balls." Maldive's voice gained strength. "I took a bunch of pills and that didn't work."

Baumholtzer looked at Maldive with a mixture of disbelief and contempt.

The waitress took the beverage amount out of the money next to Baumholtzer. Paper money that had been neatly folded, and the coins that had been stacked in diminishing size, were left in disarray. Baumholtzer set it back in order, squared his napkin, checked his tie, and centered the new pretzel basket and his drink.

Jonathan made notes. *Baumholtzer is obsessively compulsive. Maldive is suicidal.*

Baumholtzer shook his head. "When my time comes I hope it's in the courtroom. The clerk reading a not-guilty verdict is like the sweet words of a woman moaning through an orgasm."

Jonathan wrote the names of the next two people he'd transport, not liking the idea of doing a favor for one of them. Killing a criminal defense attorney who didn't have years of practice ahead didn't fit his plan. But, in Maldive's case, it would be symbolic to not let him die a natural death or on his own schedule. End Maldive's life prematurely, he thought, like his clients had ended their victims' lives. Maldive will be a garnish with Baumholtzer as the meat.

Outside The Bar, he took off his cap and pushed a hand through his hair, making it look unruly. *I look like a Greek god who's been in too many fights.* His Greek-heritage mother had told him countless bedtime stories of the tools of her gods of mythology: war, love, jealousy and, his favorite, revenge. With the name of the god he had chosen for his games of death, he'd be continuing their legends. It's only fitting, he thought.

THE ALARM SOUNDED at 3:30 a.m. Within fifteen minutes, Rush dressed, put dry cereal in a plastic bag, and drove away.

Newport Beach police had posted and handed out fliers around Corona del Mar State Beach and Balboa Pier. Newspapers had cooperated. Nothing worthy had developed.

There had to be someone near the pier or jetties who had seen something regarding the case, but out of sheer laziness, not wanting to be involved or not knowing the value of their observations, they hadn't come forward. He had to find that person. He had been here twice before, hoping to meet different groups of fishermen.

D.A. Investigator Kevin Dunley had checked Benedict's victims for criminal records and to determine if any had made threats against Benedict or Polperro. Negative. Checking Newport Beach, Costa Mesa, Huntington Beach and Laguna Beach police departments for traffic or parking citations on the morning of Polperro's death had developed no leads.

Newport Beach police had contacted all occupants in the bluff houses overlooking Corona del Mar State Beach. Many of the homes had telescopes overlooking the beach. No information.

He reviewed the law concerning the suspected murder of Polperro. Even if someone made an admission he had murdered Polperro, it couldn't come into evidence until the prosecution had first proven Polperro's death was a murder independent of the suspect's statement. So far, they had no such proof.

Rush spent an hour talking to fishermen. No leads. Walking to his car, he noticed an older man and a young boy going onto the pier. The instincts of a prosecutor made him follow.

At mid-pier he identified himself but gave no reason for the questions he'd be asking, wanting untainted replies. The boy, Roge, appeared about fourteen and the man identified himself as the grandfather, Robert Sellins.

"Have you been here before?"

The grandfather laughed. "Roge is a fishing nut." He tousled the boy's hair and beamed with apparent satisfaction.

"Good." Rush tried to make the situation as personable as possible, "Then I assume you're an expert."

Roge appeared shy. "My grandfather taught me."

"Before today, when's the last time you were here?"

"On my birthday. My grandfather surprised me with this new rod." He held it out. "Isn't it a beaut."

"You must be his pride and joy to get a gift like that." Rush's mind fleetingly raced to the fact that he had never known his own grandparents. The joy in Roge's face eased his pain. "What date is your birthday?"

Roge replied with a date in June as Rush reached into his wallet and pulled out a card calendar. The date matched the morning Polperro disappeared. "Did you see anything unusual or different that morning?"

"Like what?" asked the grandfather.

He smiled, "Anything, anything at all."

They shook their heads.

Rush asked the question a different way. "Aside from fishing, do you remember anything in particular about that morning?" Rush added, "Any particular conversations or observations, something different from the usual things you talk about, see or do." He laughed. "A clown, an airplane, a jet ski, anything."

Roge replied, "Like the diver we saw walking from the pier to the jetty?"

Rush patiently waited.

"A diver. I could make out the fins and spear gun."

"That seems ordinary to me."

"He carried what looked like a rebreather."

"What's a rebreather?" Perhaps Roge would note Rush's lack of knowledge and want to instruct him.

"The rebreather looks like a kid's backpack, just larger and maybe more square. I'm saving money to buy one."

Rush's mind raced with anticipation.

"That person had all the other diving equipment except for the cylinder, so it had to be a rebreather."

"What time did you get here that morning?"

"It wasn't sunrise yet, but there's a lot of lights on around here," the grandfather replied.

"Do you remember when you last saw him?"

"I didn't look at him again."

"The last I saw him," added the grandfather, "he was still walking toward the jetty."

JONATHAN sat in his garage and reviewed information that Baumholtzer and his wife had recently moved and were living in a condo in Irvine. Their children were attending universities in New York and Virginia.

If I plan to murder…no, wait. What I'm doing isn't a crime. It's transporting. He laughed. *I transport them to Charon, who takes them to the land of the dead. Hades will welcome them.*

The kitchen door opened behind him and he felt the warmth of Jessica's arms around his neck. He rose and held her at arm's length, "Honey, let's get a baby sitter and have a night out. We could use some quality time together."

She gave a sensual wink and swayed her hips. "What exactly do you have in mind, big guy?"

"Torrid lovemaking."

"I'd like that." She met his lips and gently pushed her tongue into his mouth.

RUSH WAITED for Ann outside the courtroom after the judge had ordered Tabbetts released on bail of one-million dollars. "How about a cup of coffee?"

"Thanks, but no, I've got appointments."

"A couple of minutes, here, now?" He tried not to sound pleading.

"Sure."

"I'm sorry about Polperro."

35

"Thanks. Anything else?"

Her reply made him wince. "Yes. I've changed a great deal since we lived together. I hired an investigator to find my parents. I accept the blame for what I did and how I acted. I…" He stopped, feeling he'd been babbling.

Ann appeared surprised but said nothing.

"May I see you again?"

She put a hand on his arm. "Rush, I'll think about it, but right now I have to go." She turned to leave.

Instinctively he grabbed her arm but let go when Ann glared. "Please, stay for just a moment."

She walked to a bench and sat against the wall.

Rush sat beside her. "Ann, your family is the only family I've ever really known. You've had everything financial and supportive handed to you on a silver platter and yet you're the most mature, level-headed person I've ever known."

"We've been through all that." Ann started to get up.

"No, please, wait. I'm sorry. I'm trying to have you understand what I've been faced with in our relationship."

"We've also been through all that. My degree from Vassar, Master's from Yale and top of my law class at Duke University, a new car every year and a new house in Turtle Rock, Irvine, all the courtesy of my wealthy parents. So what."

"Don't you realize what's been ingrained in me because of my background? Hard knocks are supposed to develop a person, but I've carried a lot of resentment I didn't want to recognize."

Ann picked up her briefcase and walked away. "Isn't that too late for us?"

ANN COULDN'T DENY her love for Rush since they had first met at a triathlon in Hawaii, before the bad memories of their last six months together. It was difficult to blame him, he had experienced a life that was difficult for her to imagine.

Rush never had the size or speed for organized sports, he had earned scholastic scholarships. In undergraduate school he entered triathlons to gain more discipline and competitiveness. By being gregarious, Rush had substituted groups and meetings for the family he never had. Hardships had built character but left him vulnerable.

Ann had enjoyed their competitiveness in triathlons and in the courtroom. Their private time finally destroyed their relationship. If only she had said *no* on that summer's day.

How strange, she thought. Polperro died on the east side of the mouth of Newport Bay. Her relationship with Rush disintegrated on the west side, at the Wedge.

SIX

Jurors, witnesses, lawyers and spectators crowded the sixth-floor hallway of the county courthouse. Sitting on a bench, Jonathan opened a newspaper and watched as Rush exited an elevator and walked to the far end of the hallway.

He must have an opinion about Polperro's death. Rush gets all the benefits of my plan without any of the risks. Good to see him up close. It'll make the telephone call seem like a face-to-face conversation. Waiting a few minutes, he stepped to the public telephones in a deserted alcove next to the elevators.

No using a wireless phone. It'd leave a traceable record if authorities ever caught him. Quickly donning a pair of latex gloves, he picked up the farthest telephone, turned his back to the entrance, dropped the coins and dialed.

"Hello?"

"I have an important message for Mr. Rushton Jones." He quickly decorated his mouth with m&m's.

The courtroom clerk held the phone in the air. "Rush?"

"Hello? Rush here."

"Hi! *Click. Click.* Isn't it a beautiful day?"

Rush tried to grasp the situation. Only his secretary ever called him in a courtroom. The caller didn't identify himself. The *clicking*, the *clicking!* He couldn't associate it with the call being recorded, nor did it sound like electrical interference. He'd wait to see if it had a pattern. Pulling a tape recorder from an inside coat pocket, he held it near the ear piece.

"Who's calling please?"

"Have your...*click*...days been going well? *Click. Click.*"

"Some days are better than others." Rush focused on ways to ferret out information on the caller and the reason for the call.

"*Click.* I know, Mr. Jones, but...*click...click*...tell me, did anything in particular...*click*...brighten your day...*click...click*... in the last month?"

"When I'm fighting *evil* all the time it's tough to find a bright day."

The caller's voice appeared lighter and understanding. "Evil...*click...click...*evil and compensation...*click...*go together. *Click.*"

No one but the killer would link evil with compensation in this conversation. "I received your letter."

Silence.

"The letter's connected to Polperro's death, isn't it?"

Jonathan shuffled his feet. Except for the last comment about *evil,* Rush's apparent neutrality didn't please him. *Maybe he's not as intelligent as I thought. Why doesn't he show satisfaction in Polperro's death? He picked up on the word* compensation. *Maybe he's talking code about my letter. We know what we're saying to each other but no one else would.*

Rush tried to avoid accusatory questions, wanting the killer to initiate admissions. He could not let the killer think he was doing a good thing or that he approved. What if the killer went on a murder spree and, after being caught, said Rush had encouraged him. What if the killer recorded this conversation?

His neutral stance could be interpreted as one where Rush failed to unequivocally disassociate himself from the killer. On the other hand, such a position could end the calls and a chance of proving murder and identifying the killer.

"Compensation for evil. The criminal justice system does as much as it can but they can go only so far. Meantime, people live, people die."

"Die. *Click.* You mean...*click...click...*like Polperro...*click?*"

"Polperro did a good job for his clients." He heard a gasp. *Damnit! Poor phrasing.* Quickly, Rush added, "But, as you know, it's mostly defense lawyers and criminals who feel that way."

Pleased, Jonathan realized Rush had to maintain a certain outward stance while he was silently cheering. The m&m's rattled against his teeth as he shifted some to the pockets of his cheeks to be able to speak distinctly and yet disguise his voice. "A...*click...*lot of Polperro's are out...*click...click...*there."

39

*   *   *

Rush was distracted by a client asking his lawyer if there were pay phones in the hallway. *How did the killer know to call me here, and at this time? I don't hear wireless-phone noise, traffic noise or noise from an outside phone's surroundings.*

"Just a moment, the court clerk wants to ask me something." Rush snatched a piece of paper off the clerk's desk and cryptically scribbled. "Killer on phone. Listen. Make excuses 4 me."

As the clerk read the note, he held the phone out to her. The bailiff announced the judge's entry, causing the clerk to turn her head. She dropped the phone against the desk top, it hit an open drawer and clattered to the floor.

Christ, that'll scare him off! Rush pushed his way through the courtroom and slammed against the doors. Racing down the hallway he arrived to see the doors closing on two elevators. One going up, the other down. If the killer was on either elevator, he could get off on any floor. *What's the point, I can't identify him.*

Frustrated, he walked into the telephone alcove. Eight m&m's were on the small counter beneath the telephone box. He held the m&m's in a loose fist and shook them as though he were ready to roll dice. *Click - click - click - click - click.* Some issues were resolved. *Polperro was murdered and the killer wants my approval.*

AT THE UNIVERSITY of California medical library, Irvine, Jonathan selected four volumes on forensics and indexed the appropriate pages on *Electrocution*. Causes of death had to be suicide or accident.

I couldn't take the chance of waiting around the telephone alcove to see if Rush were trying to capture me. Maybe I can get that out of him on some future contact.

Opening several texts, he made notes.

120 volts are more deadly if victim can't break
contact with the current.

Low voltage may have an absence of body marks.
For electrocution, I need at least 120 volts,
sufficient length of exposure, a method to
direct the current through the body,
a way to lower victim's resistance and, lastly,
hopefully eliminate victim's preparedness for shock.

Length of exposure and low resistance is
important when dealing with 120 volts. But, even
a low-voltage shock will kill someone with a
diseased heart. Baumholtzer's weight, age,
and an alcohol-diseased heart, should make electrocution
easy. Sudden death occurs if the electricity
passes through the heart or respiratory center.

Dangerous path: electricity passing through the heart
by entering the left arm and passing out through
the right leg. Electricity follows the path of least
resistance, that is, blood-filled vessels.

Wet skin increases the contact area and lowers
the victim's resistance fourfold.

He pushed back his chair and contemplated. *How do I make it look like an accident?* Thirty minutes later he had formulated his plan.

IT TOOK RUSH MORE than twenty minutes to drive five miles. The surface streets were clogged with a combination of traffic, accidents and road repairs.

Entering the dive shop, he was directed to Bill Gladstone. "Hello, Bill?" Rush showed his identification and handed him a business card. "Do you have a few minutes?"

"Of course." Gladstone motioned Rush to follow. They entered a small office to the rear of the shop and sat down. "What's up?"

"I need to know about rebreathers."

"In a nutshell, rebreathers were developed by the United States military. Exhaled carbon dioxide goes through tubes to the rebreather. A scrubbing agent removes the carbon and the diver breathes recirculated air. It extends the overall diving time and there are no telltale bubbles."

"Do all rebreathers operate without bubbles?"

"No. You have to go up in price for that feature. Rebreathers can run from thirty-five hundred to over forty thousand. A minimum good rebreather that wouldn't leave bubbles would cost in the vicinity of sixty-five hundred."

Rush blinked and smiled. "Besides the price, what else is unique?"

"A quality rebreather can give you a minimum of three hours under water. It could go up to twelve hours and even more, depending on the equipment."

"Assume a diver is underwater and wearing the sixty-five-hundred-dollar rebreather for the entire hypo I'm going to give you." He gave a brief scenario of what he thought the sequence of events were in Polperro's death. "If he stayed under the water for the entire time would he have enough air."

"Yes."

"At the rebreather prices you mentioned, I don't suppose there's one in every garage."

"I'd guess there are probably no more than fifteen privately-owned rebreathers in Orange County."

"So, every shop in the county that sold one would have an invoice with the buyer's name and address?"

He nodded. "Better than that, every shop that sells a rebreather must register the purchaser for a training course that takes several days."

"Anything else?"

"Rebreathers take a special enriched gas mixture. Even though an owner may repair his own rebreather, he'd have to come to a shop for parts, chemicals, gas and so forth. We'd have an invoice on that."

"What about the manufacturer's warranty?"

"Good point," said Gladstone. "They're all registered with the manufacturers and they could probably break them down to Orange County. That may even include those who moved into the county if the owners had had a warranty problem after they got here."

"Do you have the manufacturer's names and addresses?"

"I do. The major ones are foreign. I'll get them for you."

Rush rose and stretched. "Would you show me a rebreather in the sixty-five hundred dollar range?"

Gladstone lead him to the main showroom and pointed. "All those."

The units looked like backpacks. *At last, a break in the case.*

JONATHAN DROVE SOUTH on I-5, exited onto Culver Boulevard in Irvine, turned left onto Warner and then onto West Yale Loop. Baumholtzer lived in a triplex condo with alley garages. He drove onto a street that ended in a T intersection with the alley and parked in the right T, facing Baumholtzer's garage at the dead-end of the left T. Walking to Baumholtzer's garage, he observed an outside light-sensor fixture on the front right face of the structure, about six-and-a-half feet above the ground. A plant sat under the fixture in a five-inch deep boarded well of dirt.

With a gloved hand he unscrewed the bulb from the fixture, flashed a light and noted it was sixty watts. He had brought bulbs of three different wattage. Taking a burned-out sixty-watt bulb from a pocket, he placed it in the fixture.

At one a.m., Baumholtzer pulled into his garage, got out of his car and turned on an inside light. Taking something from a shelf, he went to the outside garage light. His right foot went into the plant well as he unscrewed the burned-out bulb with his left hand. Seconds later, a new bulb cast its light.

Jonathan smiled. Baumholtzer's obsessive compulsion would be his death.

"THE KILLER had to take Polperro by surprise and the use of a rebreather would be essential." Rush explained as Dunley settled into a chair.

"Right." Dunley got up, appearing anxious to start. "Are you aware Deputy Sheriff Sullivan of the Sheriff's Harbor Patrol and Lieutenant Briden own rebreathers?"

"No. I know Sullivan's father-in-law was a major victim in the Benedict fraud, but…" The decision was automatic as Rush paced behind his desk. "Check them out. They're suspects until we learn otherwise. If anyone tries to use their clout regarding either of them, let me know immediately."

"Of course."

Rush returned to his chair. "I'd expect the killer to have his rebreather serviced outside the county. What about the killer's letter?"

Dunley shook his head. "The paper is available in any stationery store. There's a unique aspect to the letter "t" but until we catch the killer we're not going to find the typewriter."

"Restrict your rebreather investigation to Orange County owners for the present."

Dunley left. Rush felt unsettled by the news regarding Sullivan and Briden. He trusted them but he had seen too much crime not to have a little suspicion with every trust.

Deep in thought, the ringing telephone sounded like tugboat blasts. "Hello?"

"Rush, Detective Cortez, Newport Beach. We have another dead lawyer. Sheraton Hotel. Sam Horne was found hanged in a hotel room. No apparent evidence of foul play."

"I'm leaving now."

RUSH ARRIVED at Hotel Sheraton's fifth floor, nodded to the personnel in the room and, joined by Cortez, went directly to Dr. Ben. "What do you have?"

"A Polperro-type death. No defensive wounds. Except for the belt marks on the neck there are no cuts or bruises anywhere on the body. His hands are bagged. We'll scrape the nails at the lab."

44

"Do you see anything indicating murder?"

"No. The belt was basically above the Adam's Apple. That's where it's expected to be due to the weight of the body pulling it to the jaw."

"Are the bruises consistent with a doorknob belt hanging?"

"Yes. There's no wide area of bruising or heavy bruising that'd indicate Horne was conscious, surprised from behind, and garroted. In a struggle, the belt would've moved about the neck causing bruising inconsistent with the belt width and movement in a hanging. And, the neck marks have a symmetry that's consistent with a hanging. If the killer had hanged a dead man, the neck bruises would be brown in color because there wouldn't have been any blood circulation. The bruises are red. He was alive when the belt cinched around his neck."

Rush shook his head. "Scary, isn't it."

Dr. Ben nodded. "Like Polperro. This one comes off like a bonafide suicide and yet that gut feeling tells me otherwise."

"Cortez," Rush asked, "who registered for the room?"

"Horne. The clerk who checked him in doesn't recall anyone else being with him."

"When did he check in?"

"Early evening yesterday. A Do Not Disturb sign was on the doorknob. Because of check-out time, the maid entered and found him."

"Then the door chain wasn't connected?"

"Right." Cortez followed through on Rush's thinking. "A killer wouldn't be able to connect the chain lock when he left. But, we're speculating, Horne may not have used that lock."

"What other investigation is going on?"

"We're checking out why Horne was here, there's no law convention or seminar and he owns a home in Irvine."

"Are you aware he's gay?"

"No," Cortez replied.

"That might be why he rented a hotel room, doesn't want to meet anyone he knows and doesn't want his Irvine neighbors seeing only men going in and out." Rush turned to Dr. Ben. "Do you have a theory for murder?"

"A person known and friendly to Horne, or a one-night-stand lover, for example, could apply pressure to the carotid arteries for a few seconds to render him unconscious and then hang him with the belt."

"Doorknob hanging isn't a common way of committing suicide."

"No, but it's effective. It doesn't take much pressure on the neck to die by hanging. I've seen successful suicides from a bedpost and a refrigerator door handle."

"Rush, did you get a letter on this one?" Cortez asked.

"No."

"So it could be a suicide."

Rush nodded. "Anything in the room showing evidence of a struggle? Any personal items missing, like a wallet?"

"No. It's like Horne came into a freshly made-up room and didn't disturb a thing."

Rush tried to sort things out. "Horne just finished defending a criminal child-abuse case. That's consistent with the killer's pattern. The lack of a letter bothers me. It could mean the killer isn't going to conform to a plan, that is, if there's only one killer."

WEARING GLOVES, Jonathan sat in his garage. Being a one-man judge, jury and executioner, no one could meddle with the outcome - death. He smiled, pleased with himself. Some people never find their mission in life or know what their talents are.

It's Baumholtzer time.

With strengthened resolve, he concentrated on his work.

Over a wooden replica, he shaped a sixty-watt sized bulb out of thin copper sheeting. The copper bulb fell short of the threaded neck of the bulb. He removed the insulation from both ends of a short piece of electrical wiring. One end was soldered to the top of the copper bulb. The splayed other end was curved over the top of the wooden neck to make electrical contact in the socket. The wire's insulated portion would guard against a short. The neck of the wooden bulb would provide rigidity in the socket. Lastly, he removed the excess copper from the bottom of the bulb, then crimped and hammered the remainder to a smooth, round surface.

The copper bulb looked like a bomb from a kid's cartoon. He placed it on the table and covered it. Taking a fifty-foot extension cord, he cut off the female end and left two inches of wire exposed.

Jeff entered, bouncing a basketball.

"What is it, son?"

"Shoot some baskets?"

He reached out and hugged him. "Warm up. I'll be there in a few minutes. Don't forget we're going fishing for halibut tomorrow."

He rubbed his stomach as he walked away. "How could I forget, it's my favorite."

Jonathan looked at the photo of Kurt Balmholtzer in the Los Angeles Times. The 7-11 murder trial was in its final stage. Not even Baumholtzer's death would bring the victim back to his family. "Baumholtzer, you are about to be transported to Hades."

"Honey, come on, Jeff is waiting to shoot baskets and dinner will be in twenty minutes." Jessica spoke as she entered from the kitchen.

"I'd have been out there a long time ago if I could figure out how to beat him. Jeff's really good." He laughed.

SEVEN

Baumholtzer had primed his stressed-out body with tranquilizers, trying to calm his rapid heart beat. High blood pressure felt as though it were creating a blow hole. The adrenalin of combat. Baumholtzer against the world.

A great deal of satisfaction came from getting someone acquitted whom he fully believed was innocent. But that was the exception. Most defendants had committed the act which caused them to be arrested and charged. The issue was whether or not the prosecution could prove it. Baumholtzer loved the power of having a life in his hands and convincing a jury to believe the evidence as he saw it.

He squared his tablet with the edge of the counsel table, laid his pens parallel with the edge, quickly touched his tie to be sure the knot was in place, and centered the ring on his finger.

Years peeled away. He loved the power of delivering words.

Some Other Dude Did It! The jury needs a way out of a guilty verdict. Any excuse will do, reasons aren't necessary. Call him boy, *bring out their parental instincts.*

"Ladies and Gentlemen of the jury." He succinctly went through the defense evidence. Store cameras weren't functioning. A friend of the boy had picked him up and they drove to a 7-11 store to buy soda. At the cash register, the friend unexpectedly pulled a gun. The clerk reached for a weapon, the friend fired.

The defendant covered his face, shoulders caved.

"The friend dropped the gun and ran. The clerk, mortally wounded, struggled to his feet and pointed his weapon at the boy. The frightened boy, in self defense, picked up the friend's gun and pointed it at the clerk, but didn't shoot. The clerk fell, and died. The boy's prints were now on the gun.

"He ran outside, frightened, panicking. The friend had driven away. A customer saw the boy with the gun and called police. They found him hiding nearby. He immediately gave the friend's name to the police and explained what I just told you - the same as what the boy told you when he took the stand. He did not shoot the clerk. There was only one shot and lab analysis showed no gunpowder residue on the boy's hands. The shooter is a fugitive and hasn't been apprehended."

Defendant was acquitted on the evening of the second day of deliberations.

JONATHAN TURNED off the I-5 and made his way to the Irvine main post office on Sand Canyon. The verdict was in on Baumholtzer. Guilty! Death! He stopped at the drive-up mail box and, wearing gloves, deposited a letter to Rush. Tonight, Baumholtzer would be transported.

BAUMHOLTZER BROKE FREE of the media and went to his office.

He poured scotch over ice and fell exhausted into his desk chair. The letdown, the feeling of dissolving. Hands shaking, he put his glass on the desk. Sleep took him for an hour. Awakening, he drained his glass, poured another, changed his shirt and suit and went through the ritual of squaring everything on his desk.

Entering The Bar, the drinking fraternity applauded. Baumholtzer raised a glass of scotch to the crowd and drained it.

Stephen Maldive led Baumholtzer to a table in a far corner of the lounge. Maldive's eyes were shifting. "How did you do it, Kurt?"

Baumholtzer felt uncomfortable, but his ego labored under his fourth double scotch. "The boy went in on a robbery to get some easy money. The friend had told him the gun was defective. The murder was totally outside of what he expected, wanted or would have done on his own. The boy isn't a murderer."

Maldive grabbed Baumholtzer's arm as he raised his drink. "Doesn't that bother you?! The kid went into the 7-11 to do a robbery! The death of the clerk is a reasonable and possible consequence. He's a murderer."

Baumholtzer's heart pounded as he angrily replied, "If the kid had testified he had committed the robbery with his friend but had no idea there'd be gunplay, do you think the jury would stop with a guilty verdict on the robbery and acquit him of murder? Bullshit! If *they* did the robbery, *they* did the murder. That's the way juries think."

"But...but..."

"We tried to plead to an armed robbery but the D.A. wouldn't take anything less than murder." With great satisfaction, he added, "Now the assholes got nothing."

PARKING IN THE RIGHT part of the T about midnight, Jonathan sat for ten minutes with his windows down. The coastal fog and mist of June had persisted into the summer. It dimmed the glow of the exterior garage lights. There were no unexpected sounds. He put on a pair of heavy-duty rubber gloves. Placing various items in his pockets, he exited and closed the door to the point of meeting the frame.

No condo lights were on as he crossed the T to Baumholtzer's garage. Moving quickly to the light fixture, he unscrewed the bulb and put it in a pocket. The sprinkler head, to the right of the plant under the fixture, was removed and placed in a plastic bag.

Forcing the wooden neck of the copper bulb into the socket, he felt the splayed end of wire made contact with the current. Baumholtzer's spasms mustn't pull it loose, possibly breaking the circuit before he died.

He returned to his car. Without closing the door, he emptied his pockets of everything except a burned-out bulb and the sprinkler head. Slouching in his seat, he waited.

BAUMHOLTZER'S waistline was fifty inches while above and below he looked somewhat normal in weight and build. Alcoholic beverages fueled his body but it had caused noticeable physical deterioration, making it difficult to function clearly before noon.

A liver-spotted head matched the back of his hands. He called it camouflage. His face had taken on a rosy glow with broken capillaries coloring his cheeks and nose. Compulsiveness made him dress conservatively and impeccably. A deep-sounding voice resonated with perfect diction. Witnesses and juries were never abused. They appeared to trust him.

From West Yale Loop, he entered the alley and into the T. "Shit, the light is out again!" The garage door went up. Exiting his car, he turned on the inside garage light.

Automatic sprinklers had shut off five minutes before. Baumholtzer's inside garage light went off and the garage door closed. Jonathan gasped. *What did I do wrong?* He slammed the passenger seat with his fist. "Damn! All my planning! All my dedication! Holy Zeus, what have you done to me! I've mailed the letter to Rush!"

He leaped from the car and was more than halfway to the garage when he heard the door begin to grind open. Ducking behind shrubbery at the gate to a neighbor's yard, he waited. Baumholtzer came out of the garage and went to the light fixture.

He didn't find light bulbs in the garage so he went to the house to get some. He's compulsive. That's why he turned off the light and closed the garage door even though he'd be gone for only a minute.

Baumholtzer moved unsteadily until he was under the light fixture. His right foot went into the well of water in the plant bed.

"Goddamn! My new loafers!" He stepped back onto the macadam, leaned against his car and laid the replacement bulb on the trunk's back lip. He wiped the water off his shoe with his left hand.

He stepped on the rim of the plant bed and placed his wet left hand inside the glass fixture. Normally, he'd grab the bulb at the bottom, but he was tired, drunk, and lacked muscular control.

His fingers wrapped around the copper bulb, with his palm at the bottom. A needle-thin sabre of fire passed through his body in one continuing explosion. Muscle spasms secured his grip. Electricity entered his left arm, followed the circulatory system to his heart and came out his right leg. Instant death.

Baumholtzer fell, his left hand clutching the copper bulb.

Jonathan listened, looked. All clear. He sprinted to his car and back to the garage, plugged in the extension cord, turned off the inside light and went to the body. Removing the copper bulb, he grasped Baumholtzer's left hand, folded it around a burned-out sixty-watt bulb, and placed the bulb on the trunk's back lip.

Swiftly, he applied the exposed wires of the extension cord to the tip of the left index finger. Burning flesh. A stroke of genius. Pulling the plug on the cord, he took Baumholtzer's replacement bulb off the trunk and placed it in the dirt next to the body.

He screwed the sprinkler head onto the pipe, facing the opening as before. Next, he pushed the light-fixture socket to the side.

Jonathan forced a quarter to the gum line between Baumholtzer's upper two front teeth and removed it. The ritual was complete. *You are hereby transported. Sin no more. Praise Zeus.*

Checking his property, he ran to his car, didn't close the door, and sat observing for ten minutes. Shifting to neutral, he pushed the car into motion down the slight slope. On West Yale Loop, he started the motor without gunning it, and slowly and evenly pulled away. The door was fully closed when he turned onto Culver Boulevard. He ran a hand through his hair, ruffling it.

The police might see one glaring question in the whole scene. For a fleeting moment he felt a rare rush of panic. It quickly passed. They'd have to be extra thorough to find the error.

At three in the morning, as he crawled into bed, his wife sleepily asked, "How was your meeting? What time is it?"

"Everything went well, probably after midnight." She was sleeping again before he finished his reply.

THEY WALKED UP behind him as he unlocked his car. Something cold and hard pressed against his head. Spinning around, the gun barrel bit into his forehead. "No! No! Don't!" he shouted.

They laughed, eyes furtive.

"No! No! Don't!"

The barrel moved to his left temple. Laughter. The heat and force of the discharge expanded the hole made by the bullet. Explosion debris discolored the wound. No more pleas, no more hope. Dead.

Jonathan's screams bounced against the walls. Why? Why? he asked himself as he sat up in bed, lights coming on, body shapes appearing.

Jessica hugged him. Jeff huddled the other children as he cried out, "Dad? Dad? Are you OK? Please, Dad, please tell us you're OK!" The children, frightened and crying, ran to their father.

RUSH, DR. BEN AND DUNLEY arrived within an hour of being called. County law enforcement agencies had received a confidential memo from Rush that Dr. Ben and he be immediately notified of any criminal defense attorney death in their jurisdiction.

"The wife found the body about an hour ago," said Detective Hightower, Irvine Police Department, as he looked at the entourage and added, "this is too much brass for what looks like an accident."

Rush related the gist of the Polperro and Horne cases.

"If the public knew someone was killing criminal defense attorneys, they'd simply say, 'So what's the problem?'" He didn't smile.

"It's a state of mixed emotions for some people, but we don't have that problem, do we?"

"Definitely not," was the unflinching reply, "I guess it's too early for humor."

Rush went to the body, motioning for the video cameraman to follow and record everything.

Dr. Ben kneeled. "This is fascinating. His left index fingertip has what appears to be an electrical burn."

Hightower was puzzled. "Electrical? You can tell it isn't - say - a match burn?"

"It's possible," replied Dr. Ben, "and depends on the length of time of contact. An electrically burned area is dry and charred, showing a grayish-white ulcer-like opening with corrugated margins and necrosed tissue. It's devoid of the usual inflammation and the red line of demarcation as seen in ordinary burns. It appears electricity entered at the tip of the index finger, flattening the skin ridges. The finger-tip pattern in the burned area will be lost. I'll get a better view in the autopsy room."

"Baumholtzer was lefthanded and a functioning alcoholic," said Hightower, "I've cited him on driving violations."

"Look at this." Dr. Ben shined a light on Baumholtzer's left palm. "There appears to be a faint redness on some of his fingers below the tips and across the palm."

"Signifying what?" asked Rush.

"I'm not sure. I'm mentioning it because it's an unusual marking, it has a line. Nothing here should have caused it."

"A line?"

"The redness on the palm ends somewhat abruptly, like a line drawn across near the bottom of the palm. If Baumholtzer had accidentally placed his left index fingertip into the socket, I don't see why he has burns on the fingers and palm of the same hand. Strange," Dr. Ben mused.

Rush shined a light into the fixture. "The socket's askew. It's possible he couldn't find the socket opening and may have tried to locate it with his finger. Instead of hitting the socket rim, his finger went into it. It's a possible scenario if he was drunk."

Rush checked the bulb resting on the back edge of the car trunk. Sixty watts. Filaments scrambled on the inside when he tilted it. He checked the unbroken bulb on the ground. Seventy-five watts and it appeared sound.

He flashed his light on the plant bed under the fixture. "The amount of water seems excessive. No sprinkler heads appear to be missing in this area. The other side of the alley is

54

reasonably dry. Baumholtzer probably moved to the right so he could reach into the fixture with his left hand. If that's so, why is his left index fingertip burned instead of his right?"

Dr. Ben queried, "What are you getting at?"

"Baumholtzer was lefthanded. If he were putting in a new bulb and trying to locate the socket opening, wouldn't he have the new bulb in his left hand while he used his right hand to locate the socket opening? The burn should be on his right index finger."

"That makes sense," Dr. Ben replied, adding, "OK, here's a preliminary. Baumholtzer has some classic electrocution appearances. The face is calm, the eyes congested and pupils are dilated. When you approximate the time he was electrocuted, his current rigor mortis and post-mortem lividity will support death by electrocution because those aspects develop faster in electrocution deaths. Electrocution appears to be the cause of death. If it's murder, how do we prove that?"

Rush answered methodically. "Along with the answer we'll get about the burn on the palm, the wetness of the area and possibly the burn on the wrong index finger, I expect to have a letter. And, I'm sure the killer will be calling me."

RUSH FELT A GENTLE shaking, sat up, and covered his face with his hands. He had gotten to his office at seven a.m. and had fallen asleep at his desk.

"God, I hate growing old." Taking his hands from his face, he looked at the clock. Nine. "I used to be able to function well without sleep for two days. Now I can't even get a fresh start at four in the morning."

"Fresh start?" Jane smiled, "what time last night did you stop working on the Tabbetts' case before you were called on Baumholtzer's death? No one can take that pace." She put the mail on his desk. "Would you like anything?"

"No, thanks."

His gloved hands reluctantly went through the stack. The existence of a second anonymous letter would establish a serial killer. *But where does Horne fit in? Maybe he doesn't. Maybe he got tired of living a double life.* Rush had seen enough murders involving family members, dopers and robbers. Though he couldn't accept that kind of behavior, it was part of any social structure. But the Polperro and Baumholtzer's deaths were so deliberate, calculating and warped, it belonged even less in a civilized society.

Two-thirds of the way through the stack, he saw it. No return address, Irvine postmark, yesterday's date. He slit the envelope along the top edge and took out the letter.

To do injustice is more disgraceful than to suffer it.
Plato, Gorgias

Deciphering the quotation came easily. In the mind of the murderer, Baumholtzer *did* an *injustice* when he got an acquittal on the 7-11 murder. Next thought. Baumholtzer was murdered. That's a *disgrace* Baumholtzer *suffered - than to suffer it.* Baumholtzer was the *doer* of the first and greater *disgrace* and the person who *suffered* the second and lesser *disgrace.*

We have a serial killer, he concluded. Both letters were postmarked within twenty-four hours of the deaths, from the city in which the murder was committed. Both killings occurred from the same day to two days after both victims had won acquittals on major criminal cases. But what about Horne?

We have a serial killer, he thought, who thinks he's the savior of the criminal justice system. He ridiculed himself for his fleeting thought: *It can't be that easy.*

The telephone rang with an ear-piercing loudness he attributed to his tiredness and anxiety.

He shouted. "Hello!"

"This is Jane. A man is on the phone. I did my best to get the usual information. No luck. He insists on talking to you. It may be your man."

Rush didn't want to take the call. Fatigue had shortened his patience and could blunt his ability to handle it. Wearily, he said, "Put him through," as he turned on the recording device.

"Hello? This is Rush, may I help you."

* * *

"Click...click...click..." Jonathan adjusted the m&m's in his mouth. "Good morning,...click...Mr. Jones. *Click. Click.*"

"Please," Rush's voice was unhurried, "call me Rush, everyone does."

Jonathan liked that. Rush was recognizing his contributions to society. *"Click...*I trust you had a...*click...click...click...* satisfactory morning...*click.*"

"I was busy at a murder scene."

"Baum...*click*...holtzer?"

No one except law enforcement or the killer would know that at this point. *Now, tread carefully.* "Yes, what do you think about that, Mr...?"

"Click. Click. Click. The problem is with the...*click...* Criminal Injustice System. *Click. Click.* I know you can't...*click*...congratulate...*click*...me for the fine job...*click*... I'm doing. Equally so, you...*click...click...click*...know I can't spell...*click*...out the details of my activities. *Click. Click. Click.* It's just nice...*click*...to talk with you. *Click ...click.* I don't feel...*click...click*...click...all alone out...*click*...here just as I... *click*...know how you feel...*click*...click...*click...click...*" He shifted the m&m's.

Two lawyers, maybe three, have been murdered and I have to walk the line. If I alienate him, the cases will be more difficult to solve. "Since you won't tell me your name I'll call you Mr. Justice." That wouldn't sit well with many people if they heard the tape, but Rush felt it'd inflate the killer's ego. "Do you expect to kill all the criminal attorneys?"

"If I transported...*click...click*...only ten would...*click*...that mean...*click*...I wasn't successful? Defendants would have to die by the hundreds. *Click.* One criminal defense attorney dead means...*click...click*...no more acquittals...*click...click*... on five or more...*click*...defendants over his lifetime. *Click. Click. Click.* Simple math. *Click. Click. Click.* Maybe I'll start a stampede to civil practice. *Click. Ha! Ha!*"

57

Rush noted the killer's use of the word *transport* instead of *kill, waste, murder* or *eliminate.* "Mr. Justice, it seems we have a lot to talk about. Let's meet."

Jonathan bit his tongue to keep from agreeing. The request made him suspicious. "*Click.* What happened that…*click…*day I called you in…*click…click…click…*the courtroom?"

"Oh, an attorney bumped into me. By the time I retrieved the phone you were gone."

"For now,..*click…click…*I'll accept that explanation."

"What about Horne?"

"What about…*click…*him?"

"You didn't send me a letter. Was it your handiwork?"

"Does it matter…*click…click…*?"

"I'm just trying to keep the correct box score."

"Did…*click…*Dr. Ben find evidence…*click…*Horne was murdered?"

"No."

"*Click…click…*well then."

"Why are you doing this?"

"*Click…*I must go. I'll be talking to you again…*click…click.*"

"When?" said Rush. "After another criminal defense attorney dies?"

"Can you think…*click…click…*of a better time?

EIGHT

"What did you find?" he asked with a dry voice. After a lifetime of thinking about his mother and father, and never making an effort to find them for fear of making his personal life and memories worse, Rush had reached a threshold.

Broxton held out a large brown envelope. "I believe this is your birth certificate."

He made no effort to take it. It would mean that all he had lived had been a meaningless passage of time waiting for this moment. *Here's your birth date, mother and father. Start your life over.*

Broxton laid the envelope on the coffee table. "Searching through *Joneses* didn't seem the way to go. I checked for *Rushton Fowlers* and came up with six nationwide. Looking at the probable current age of your father, western location, and other related matters, I eliminated five and struck pay dirt." Looking comfortable on the large ottoman, he appeared to wait for a reaction. None.

"I went to the county seat in Montana where this particular Rushton Fowler lives and got a photocopy of a birth certificate for a Rushton Fowler Jones. Your mother appears to be Peggy Sue Jones."

"My mother's surname is my last name?"

He nodded. "There's a plausible explanation."

"Yes?" He nervously glanced at the envelope, still not feeling confident enough to pick it up.

"Assuming Peggy Sue Jones is your mother, she became pregnant by Rushton Fowler, they had a falling out and didn't marry. The Joneses in that area appear to be financially lower class. Rushton Fowler's parents probably looked upon her as unsuitable - lack of education, no money or social standing, and so forth - for their only son and future owner of their vast estate. Your mother probably felt her surname would be more appropriate than the name of a man who wouldn't stand on his own two feet."

Rush struggled with the information. His voice filled with pride. "Sounds like the kind of mother I'd like to have. Can you tie in this particular Rushton Fowler as my father?"

"Circumstantially, yes. I didn't want to get too inquisitive around town where your mother had lived and possibly have it get back to Rushton Fowler before you and I talked. Any questions so far?"

"No."

Broxton shifted his weight on the ottoman. "About your mother, Peggy Sue Jones was a beautifully tall and capable young girl. She worked at the Fowler ranch, handling horses. The ranch is now owned and operated by Rushton Fowler, sixth-generation ownership, and is one of the biggest in Montana. There are three sisters, your aunts, none of whom live locally. Rushton Fowler would have been about five years older than Peggy Sue.

"The rest is supposition. Your mother gave you her surname but in defiance to the the Fowler family she gave you the father's first and last names. She took you away, couldn't give you the support you needed, left you on the doorstep of an orphanage and disappeared. I haven't found anything on Peggy Sue Jones in any of the counties surrounding that area in Colorado. The immediate decision concerns Montana. You or I have to personally meet Rushton Fowler."

Rush raced the issues through his mind with the same speed and objective elimination he used in a courtroom. "I want answers from Rushton Fowler. But, between a serial killer and the Tabbetts' case, I can't take the time now. You go, and let it all hang out."

Broxton exerted great effort to get off the low ottoman. They shook hands. "You won't regret bringing the past into your future."

Rush looked at the envelope for a long time before he opened it. *Finally, a birthday party on the correct day.* The humor of that told him he had conquered his initial anxieties.

KEVIN DUNLEY didn't like knowing Kurt Baumholtzer was probably murdered and yet not being able to reveal that fact to his widow.

She appeared nervous as she moved the cookies closer to him and poured the coffee. "I don't understand why you're here."

"I know. An accident is an accident."

"Yes."

"Mrs. Baumholtzer…"

Smiling, "Please, call me Mrs. B."

He removed two bubble-wrapped light bulbs from a paper bag and held them out. "One is seventy-five watts, the other is sixty. Did your husband put in any bulb whenever one burned out?"

"No. Heavens no." She gave that nervous laugh that grieving people often have. A natural cover up of wanting to cry.

"Kurt was compulsive, a perfectionist. When his friends kidded him about it, his reply was 'being compulsive is good. The real question is, do you do compulsive well?'" Both laughed. "He thought that was funny, too. It made him a terrific trial lawyer."

"How does that apply to the bulbs?"

"He kept a supply of sixties in the garage for the outside fixture. A couple of weeks ago he decided to use seventy-five watts, so he bought four of them."

"So it's consistent the burned-out bulb was sixty with a new supply of seventy-five watts as replacements?"

"No, I don't think that's so." She appeared to mentally sort things out before continuing. "He was compulsive. If he thought we needed seventy-five watts he'd put one in as soon as he purchased them, whether or not the sixty had burned out."

Dunley's heart quickened. "Did you see him replace the bulb?"

"He had me come out and look at the seventy-five brightness."

"Then the burned-out sixty-watt bulb we found on the trunk lid couldn't have come from the garage fixture."

"How could it?"

"You said he keeps extra bulbs in the garage for that fixture?"

"Normally, yes. But I found the package of seventy-five watts in the pantry. There were no extra bulbs in the garage, so the sixty couldn't have been in the fixture."

"He hadn't gotten around to storing the seventy-fives in the garage?"

"No," she laughed, "compulsive Kurt missed that one."

"Where are the seventy-fives now?"

Mrs. B left the room, returned with a paper bag, and handed it to Dunley. He took out two seventy-fives in one container, a second container, empty, for two seventy-fives, and a receipt for the purchase.

Dunley had Mrs. B initial and date each item in the bag and the bag itself as he offered a scenario regarding the bulbs. "Let's assume the first seventy-five he put into the garage fixture came from this bag. If that bulb had burned out on the night of his death, he'd have to get another seventy-five. That'd be consistent with finding these remaining two. So, the burned out bulb from the trunk should have been a seventy-five, not a sixty."

"That's the only way it could have gone."

"Have you put another bulb in the fixture? If so, why does the bag have two left instead of one?"

"Police told me to keep the fixture as it was, so I haven't even put a bulb in it. May I light up the area now?"

"Of course. Mrs. B, have you ever known the plant bed under the outside garage light to fill with water from the sprinklers?"

"Never. I check the plants and do trimming because the association gardeners don't keep it up the way I like it. Mr. Dunley, are you going to tell me why you're asking all these questions?"

"We like to be thorough, Mrs. B." Dunley finished his cold coffee, and asked if he might take the half-eaten cookie with him. Mrs. B wrapped all of them for his office.

RUSH PUSHED his experience and imagination down every possible investigative avenue. He took the obvious straight-forward facts of the deaths of Polperro, Horne and Baumholtzer, sifted through the killer's calls, and came up with basic points, areas of similarity, and conclusions. Many successful prosecutions came from the slimmest ideas being diligently pursued.

He contacted experts in sociology, ancient history, anthropology, philosophy, archeology and any other subject he thought might have a clue about the killer. Dr. Franklin Zald, an expert on Greek mythology, teaching at the University of California, Los Angeles, was the next contact.

After identifying himself and obtaining agreement the conversation would be held in the strictest confidence, Rush related facts concerning the murders. "In summary, the murders are committed in darkness, or night, in private. They appear to be accidents or suicide. We have *night, stealth, cunning*, the use of the word *transport* instead of murder or kill, the reference to a failed criminal justice system and the anonymous letters with a Greek or Roman quotation."

The only time Zald didn't hum some part of a Beethoven symphony was when he replied to Rush's comments. "This may sound far out but speculation doesn't seem to bother either of us."

"Shoot." Rush drummed his fingers, feeling relaxed because of Zald's humming.

"Greek mythological gods had a god as their messenger. Zeus appointed a god, Hermes, as messenger to Hades. Along with stealth, darkness and cunning, we should add the word *tricks*."

"Explain."

"With Hermes, tricks carries a distinctive punch."

"Sounds interesting."

"Hermes is the messenger god, he might be your killer's alter ego. Hermes was also the god of thieves, their good-luck charm, because he was full of tricks and cunning. Being also the god of travelers, he used his magic rod to stupefy men while he practiced magic and deception, even thievery." Humming.

"It fits. Please continue."

"You'll like this. Hermes *transported* the souls of the dead to the underworld. In that regard he appeared to be known as Psychopompos and used his magic rod when acting in that capacity. He was a deity of gain, whether honest or dishonest." Humming.

Rush waited.

"Charon was the boatman who ferried the souls of the dead across the river Styx, which separated the land of the living from the land of the dead. Charon had to be paid for his work."

"And?"

"The family or friends of the dead would wedge a silver coin between the teeth or place it under the tongue of the dead person to pay Charon for transporting the dead. Has the killer left a coin between the teeth or in the mouth?"

"No. He wants the deaths to appear as suicide or accident."

"You might think about that. If this killer, Hermes, is so fastidious in his killing schemes, he may be carrying out the coin legend in a way that hasn't yet come to your attention."

"HERMES IS THOROUGH," Rush told Dr. Ben, "I'm chancing he completes the ritual of being Hermes by inserting the coin and taking it out. We can't afford to pass any possible lead. We'll exhume the bodies and check for striations and or chips on the front teeth."

"Does that include Horne's body?"

"Yes. Three will give us a better pattern if the pattern is there."

"Will do. Meanwhile, regarding Baumholtzer, a charge of electricity went through his body, causing ventricular fibrillation. His blood pressure has been very high for years and he had an enlarged heart. The amount of alcohol in his blood would have killed anyone who hadn't built up a tolerance as he had. Baumholtzer's prints were on both bulbs."

"Was his left hand index-finger print on the burned-out bulb?"

"Yes. Like you, I hoped the killer would've made the mistake of putting Baumholtzer's left hand on the bulb *after* he had burned his index finger. That print wouldn't have taken."

"What about the red palm?"

"Part of the palm and portions of the fingers look as though they had been subjected to heat that was strong enough to cause a redness but not strong enough to cause an electrical burn. It doesn't fit anything in the electrocution evidence or scene, but, it could have come from being subjected to an electrical charge. We just have to find a scenario that fits it. Irvine police are checking that out."

"And Horne?"

"No attack debris under his nails. Only Horne's prints were on the belt. Death was due to asphyxiation. I don't have any manner of death to change that to murder."

"OUR RECORDS SHOW no calls about malfunctioning water systems, flooding, or other problems anywhere near or around the Baumholtzer condo. I also checked our requests to the landscaping contractor for repairs or for invoices regarding such problems. There are none. Everything has been in order for at least three months before the death." The property manager of the association where Baumholtzer lived had researched Dunley's questions.

The only reasonable conclusion, Dunley thought, was that the sprinkler head had been removed before the murder and then replaced. The killer had set up the death, watched it happen and put the scene back in order.

RUSH EXPLAINED to Detectives Cortez and Hightower what the name Hermes meant and how it fit into the killings, gave them tapes of Hermes' phone calls and a photocopy of the two anonymously-written letters. "The envelopes and writing paper had no identifiable prints other than those who handled them in the normal course of business."

Dunley explained the rebreather evidence, then spread papers on his lap. "Contacting all the dive shops in the county, I got seven owners' names and addresses. Included in the seven are Lieutenant Briden, Santa Ana PD and Deputy Sullivan, Orange County Sheriff's Office. I also got an additional three names and addresses of people who had purchased parts or the special gas mixture that a rebreather needs."

Cortez turned to Rush. "Did you pick up any speech patterns indicating Hermes was Sullivan or Briden?"

"It's difficult to tell. Let's do the investigation and talk about it when we have more data. There could be more names involved. An owner may have loaned his rebreather to a diving-enthusiast friend. Some may have moved into our county and have not yet had reason to seek parts or equipment."

When everyone left, Rush sat and buried his face in his hands. It helped him concentrate. Should he notify the newspapers and the bar association of the two murders and possibly Horne as a third? He couldn't defend keeping this a secret on the basis of not compromising the investigation. If he didn't go public and another murder occurred he'd be justifiably criticized. On the other hand, going public may make Hermes angry, ending the calls and whatever chance Rush had to identify and arrest him. Would publication turn Hermes into a blatant cold-blooded killer in his anger at Rush?

There were no alternatives or options to his clear-cut decision.

"HELLO?" The telephone ring sounded like a bullhorn at one in the morning. *Another attorney murder?*

"Hi, Rush, now we'll...*click*...have time to...*click*...talk. No games."

I have an unlisted number. Who the hell is this guy?

Turning on the recorder, Rush steadied his thinking and spoke with a friendly voice. "Good morning, Hermes, how are you?" No reaction. *This guy is really into self-control. Be aggressive. Get him thinking he should answer my questions to keep his credibility.* "Why didn't you leave a coin in Polperro's, Horne's and Baumholtzer's teeth, or under the tongue?"

Hermes sounded neither shocked nor surprised. "You... *click...click...*do your homework...*click...*Rush. But then... *click...*that's why I picked you. *Click. Click. Click. Click.* Do you...*click...*accept what I'm doing?"

"You're a thorough person but you're making mistakes."

"Mistakes? Like what?...*click...*" The voice sounded disturbed, as though Rush were mocking him.

Rush related the bruises on Polperro's arms, the wattage, burned index finger and the sprinkler head issues regarding Baumholtzer, and explained his reasoning. "And, we're still checking out the red palm."

No comment.

"We found all three attorneys had a hard object forced between the upper two front teeth and then removed."

Silence.

"You're playacting makes a farce out of your mission."

"You're talking like...*click...* you want me to get...*click...* caught. Anyway, I'll never...*click...click...*be taken alive."

"I disagree with what you're doing."

"Come on, *click...click...click...*you have to take that stance...*click...click...click...*but between you and me,...*click...* tell me deep down you wish me well. *Click. Click.*"

Rush's patience diminished. The Tabbetts case filled his mind and he despised people who thought they could outwit the system - even though some actually did. "Why do you refuse to accept that what you're doing is wrong?"

"Rush,...*click...*you're confusing me."

"You're murdering people and I'm confusing you?" Rush drummed his fingers on the Tabbetts' file.

"I'm making...*click...*the system work better. *Click. Click.*"

"Don't you see the incongruities in your actions?"

"Wh...*click...*at?"

"Socially acceptable behavior doesn't need death, cover of night or stealth? It degrades your acts and their purpose."

Hermes' voice had a sharp edge. "You...*click*...don't understand. They're...*click*...wayward mortals. *Click. Click. Click.* Stealth, tricks and...*click*...*click*...darkness is all they know. *Click. Click.* Hermes adds color and satisfies the gods. *Click.* Lawyers are presumed guilty."

"I repeat, what do you think you're accomplishing?"

His voice became loud and threatening. "Damnit! Don't...*click*...*click*...you ever look at the faces...*click*...of the victims' families? Their lifetime...*click*...of grief?" His voice suddenly calmed. "Those lawyers...*click*...*click*...*click*...aren't worth a plug nickel. *Click.* I hope Charon gets...*click*...*click*...*click*...mad as hell and just dumps them...click...in the Styx when he doesn't find silver. *Click. Click.*"

Hermes' raucous laugh caused Rush to take the phone from his ear. "Don't choke on your m&m's, Hermes. Other attorneys will fill the void. There'll be more acquittals."

"Don't choke on...*click*...my m&m's...*click*...? So, you didn't accidentally drop the...*click*...*click*...*click*...phone in the courtroom, you came looking for me in the telephone alcove...*click*...*click*...*click*...you found the m&m's."

Rush couldn't hide his mistake. Change the subject. "You can't be killing on a whim or out of indignation, that would be too general to put you on this road. Something personal happened to you or a loved one. It changed your life, causing you to do this. Tell me about it, I've been through this with hundreds of families."

Hermes responded with so much anguish in his voice Rush couldn't decipher a single word. The voice was so incoherent he knew it couldn't even be deciphered by an expert. He waited, knowing he had hit a nerve, hoping Hermes would calm down and talk about it.

Instead, Hermes picked up on their previous topic and his voice turned more clear and ominous. "I'll have more...*click*...lawyers to kill when others fill the void. *Click. Click. Click.*" The clicking lost its sharpness. The m&m's were melting.

"Why don't we meet, you choose the place and time. I promise no heroics. We can talk this out."

Rush heard a chewing, crunching and swallowing and then the rattle of fresh m&m's against the teeth.

"*Click. Click.* I'm disappointed...*click*...in you." *Click. Click.* A sharp, loud tone. "Maybe I'll add indifferent and soft...*click*...*click*...*click*...prosecutors to my list. *Click.* It's inevitable, Rush, we're going to...*click*...meet face to face. I'll know you but you...*click*...won't know me. *Click...Click... Click.*" Disconnection.

The threat angered and startled Rush. Hermes was a sociopathic killer. He actually believed murdering attorneys was the right thing to do. He's certainly intelligent. *And now, for whatever reasons he chooses, I could be on his list.*

Hermes was displeased with many of Rush's comments, but he wanted to explain why he was transporting lawyers. If he had, perhaps Rush would remember his experiences and sympathize with him, giving him more support. However, he was concerned he might leave a clue that would enable Rush to trace and identify him.

The one case that was the basis for his plan and his pain was one Rush would never know, unless he told Rush about it some day when he decided to transport him.

NINE

Courtrooms made Rush feel proud and angry, exhilarated and depressed, clean and dirty, the natural consequence of being an objective, experienced prosecutor. Fortunately, in the Tabbetts case, Judge Goldensmith will give the parties a fair trial, without courtroom theatrics, failures or weaknesses, allowing Rush to concentrate on his case.

Ann arrived before the jurors and took her seat at the counsel table. "Any news on your parents?"

"Broxton found a Rushton Fowler and a Peggy Sue Jones in Montana, along with my birth certificate. He's trying to connect it."

"I'm happy for you." She smiled, nodded and turned away, as though their past remained off limits.

Ann was aware Tabbetts' ability to hire her was directly proportionate to either a not-guilty verdict, a guilty verdict less than murder, or, as applicable, a lenient sentence. She'd do her best to sell the judge, media, jury and witnesses on the suspect's innocence because the trial was a marketplace for buying and selling, the ultimate in buyer-jury beware. The quality of packaging the defendant outweighed the quality of his guilt or innocence. Unfortunately, Tabbetts looked antiseptic. After much discussion, he had finally agreed not to bring a nail file into the courtroom.

While a prosecutor, Ann had joined major social, community and athletic clubs, using her membership to meet and entertain lawyers from major civil-law firms. She expressed her intention of going into criminal defense work. Her suggestion made sense that they turn their criminal cases over to her. Their major civil-law clients wouldn't be seeing their lawyers representing criminals, thereby avoiding a public relations problem.

"Mr. Jones, call your first witness."

Rush called Steve Ost, medical technician, hoping to get the jury to focus on personally disliking the defendant.

"Mr. Ost, tell the jury what you saw regarding Robbie's physical condition as you tried to revive him."

Ost paused. His jaw appeared to set, followed by a perceptible swallow, as if he had to separate his feelings from what he'd say. "Robbie had bruises over most of his body." Ost sipped a glass of water, as though washing down his personal pain.

"In all my years as an emergency medical technician, I've never seen such a battered..."

Ann objected. "The question has to do with what he saw, not comparison opinions."

"Sustained."

"Did you remove Robbie's diaper?"

"Yes." Ost hesitated. "His entire body was battered and bruised."

He swallowed many times in rapid succession. His face sagged.

"Without identifying each bruise on the body, were they of different colors?"

"Yes."

"Was Robbie pronounced dead at the hospital?"

"Yes, but for all practical purposes he was dead at his house."

Rush went through an item by item rundown of Tabbetts' indifference to the plight of his son. "No further questions Your Honor."

"Ms. Cavanaugh?" the judge asked, "cross?"

Ann wore a navy-blue suit with muted stripes. Her black hair enhanced her tanned skin and red lips. She had the confidence to handle her attractiveness, and, her professional conduct would be transferred to her client.

The main purpose of cross would be to keep the jury from concentrating on the defendant.

"Mr. Ost, did you at any time hear Michelle Tabbetts say my client had beaten or struck Robbie?"

"No."

"Did Mr. Tabbetts say he had beaten Robbie?"

"No."

"Did you ask him what had happened?"

"No."

"Could Mr. Tabbetts have been quiet and reclusive in order to let you do your job?"

"Objection, calls for speculation."

"Sustained."

"Mr. Ost, have you ever seen Mr. Tabbetts before that morning?"

"No."

"Then you don't know whether he is the kind of man who withdraws when a personal family tragedy occurs?"

"I do not."

"And you do not know if, at the house, he was in such shock from grieving he was unable to function?"

"I do not."

"And you do not know if he was possibly grieving much more than another person who might be outwardly showing sincere and heartfelt grief?" An indirect swipe at Michelle.

"I do not know."

"Different people show grief in different ways, do they not?"

"Yes."

"Neither do you know that at the age of ten Mr. Tabbetts had the unfortunate experience of witnessing his..."

Rush objected, "Counsel is asking this witness if..."

Goldensmith interrupted. "It may or may not be relevant further down the road, but it is not an appropriate question to ask this witness at this time."

Ann smiled and looked at the jury. "Of course, Your Honor, another time. No further questions."

The trial concluded for the day. Rush, showing uneasiness, asked Ann, "Can you spare about an hour or so for a meeting?" Ann appeared perplexed and Rush quickly added, "It concerns your safety."

Closing her briefcase, her head jerked up. "My safety! What..."

"I'm holding a press conference. You need to be there."

RUSH DIRECTED ANN to a closed-off area adjoining a conference room, from where she'd be able to hear any discussion.

Facing the reporters in the conference room, Rush went directly to the issue. "Gentlemen, thank you for coming. We need your help to catch a serial killer. You will not be given all the facts. We don't want the usual kooks confessing.

"The phrase *Trust me* should be appropriate. Here's the story you can print. Criminal defense attorneys Franco Polperro, Sam Horne and Kurt Baumholtzer were murdered." He knew he was stretching it regarding Horne but it would make the criminal defense bar more alert.

Reporters scribbled furiously. "So the deaths weren't from drowning, hanging and electrocution?"

"Those were the causes, cleverly staged by Hermes." Rush explained the mythology of the name and how it fit the crimes.

"Criminal defense attorneys are his target."

"So what's the crime?" a reporter chuckled, "our readers will keep a running box score and even suggest names for Hermes' list."

They laughed and nodded their heads. One voice thundered, "This is Orange County. I'll give a hundred-to-one odds Hermes is a Republican!"

"Gentlemen, let's stop the jokes and get back on track. The murders will continue until Hermes is caught."

The Times asked, "You want us to spread the word?"

"Yes. We'll also notify local and state bar associations."

"These are Orange County murders, why spread it over the state?" The question came from the Orange County Register.

"Hermes is a nut, and I'd appreciate it if you'd quote me. Hermes is a nut. Who knows if Hermes will stop at criminal lawyers versus civil lawyers or judges or if he'll restrict himself to this county. Who knows whether we'll start getting copy-cat killers."

Rush looked around. "That's all. You have filler from the original stories." He pondered whether to ask readers to identify anyone they know who owns or uses a rebreather. No.

If Hermes had purchased or borrowed a rebreather, the owner's life would be in jeopardy and he'd lose his most promising lead.

"Do you know who the next victim may be?"

"If the killer follows the Polperro, Horne and Baumholtzer scenarios, go through the court calendar and take your pick."

A reporter blurted, "My God! The Tabbetts case. Ann!"

Reporters left, Ann came into the conference room, sat, and nervously stretched, appearing shaken. Rush had never seen her like that, and held her stare. "In confidence, may I give you the additional facts?"

She nodded.

He gave her copies of the letters from Hermes, explained their relevancies, and detailed the evidence tending to prove the deaths as murder.

"So I'm Hermes next victim?"

"Most likely."

"You think Hermes will contact you when the story breaks and angrily say things that may help identify him?"

"I'll take any lead I can get, but there's been nothing positive so far except for the few things I mentioned. I can no longer justify keeping the murders secret."

"And I'm not a dead lawyer because I wasn't in a major criminal case since Hermes started his campaign?"

"That's what I believe."

"But why didn't he pick me, or some other attorney, instead of Horne?"

"You're forgetting Horne had completed a child-molestation case a day or so prior to his death. Horne was naked and gay. Hermes apparently wanted to prejudice the public even more against criminal defense attorneys. He'll savor your death as a crowning achievement now that the public and newspapers will be involved."

Ann appeared bewildered.

Rush's voice labored. He swallowed, not knowing how she'd take his next comment. "Don't operate on the assumption Hermes will wait until *after* the Tabbetts verdict."

"Why do you say that?"

"The nature of the criminal mind is to be more dramatic, chancy, confident, the further he goes in his killings. Hermes can continue to do things with a flair if he kills before the verdict when the victim is probably not expecting anything to happen."

"Will he act even if Tabbetts is convicted?"

Rush answered with a constricted voice. "Yes. He kills with the trial as a focal point, knowing the public's attention will be on the defense attorney. It's the defense attorney's profession, his acquittal record, the nature of the crimes he's involved in, not just how one case turned out. He'll think he has the public looking forward to reading box scores."

"Acquittal just makes the killings more sweet?"

"Correct."

"Hermes is going to kill me regardless of the outcome of this case because of my track record?"

Rush nodded.

"Either way, I'm your bait." It wasn't a question.

"That isn't fair, Ann, I didn't arrange it this way."

"Sorry." She shrugged. "This is a little overwhelming." Rush made no reply and Ann continued. "But then, what are friends for, right?"

He felt she wasn't being snide or trying to hurt him. Humor was her way to keep the subject from weighing heavily on them both. "Ann, I'd rather you didn't express it that way. I'm trying to save your life."

She nodded and came to the edge of her seat. "What's your plan?"

"Irvine and Newport Beach police will place officers inside your home for the duration of this trial. Concealed officers will be on the outside. When you're away from home you're on your own."

"Once the story breaks you think he may even start killing without relation to a specific trial or case?"

"Right, but if it's any consolation, Hermes doesn't want to get caught. Killing you in public won't be to his advantage. He'll stick to killing by stealth, cunning, and probably at night.

He still wants the aura of Hermes' mythology to keep the public more interested."

Her shrug showed a tone of inevitability. "OK."

Neither spoke. Ann got up.

Rush reached out and took her hands. Now or never. "Ann, I want to apologize. I did some pretty stupid things when I should have known better…"

"Like what, Rush?" She wondered if he had finally stopped feeling sorry for himself and would talk specifics.

"You know the…" He hesitated.

"Say it, Rush. Lay it out. Let me hear it." No compromising tone.

Ann's abrupt confrontation took away the hurdles his emotions had to cross. "I asked you to body surf at the Wedge when only a nut would go into the water in that storm."

The Wedge was a body surfer's paradise on the west side of the west jetty at the mouth of Newport Bay. A storm off Baja California brought huge waves onto south-facing beaches. They'd hit the jetty, bounce off and join the power of a large wave that hadn't been deflected. Only an experienced body surfer, ready to accept serious injury or death, would consider going in. The water could twist a surfer like a pretzel and body-slam him to the ocean floor.

"You're fudging. You didn't *ask*, you tried to *intimidate* me. And? For starters, Rush, tell me about *Antsy*."

"Every time you were reluctant to shoot the white waters at their height, ski headlong through a forested area, or accept foolhardy athletic challenges, I'd start calling you *Ann C* and then corrupt it to *Antsy* as a way of intimidation. I was controlling."

His frankness appeared to surprise her. Ann took her hands from his and walked away. Turning, she said, "You never intimidated me. I had it up to my neck with machismo men and I wanted you to know whatever you could do I could do better - or at least as well. Is it your investigation to find your parents that's making you own up to all this?"

His confidence increased. "I know who my mother and father are. I may be seeing them within a month." She appeared sincerely affected by his candidness. "It washed away a part of me that has been in limbo ever since I was old enough to realize I had no parents, no family. It had made me angry and antagonistic, not caring if I lived or died. I'm a survivor who didn't care about surviving."

"Great! If you want to stupidly challenge mother nature go jump off a cliff but don't try to drag someone with you. Did I ever change your name from *Rushton* to *Rush in* because you always seem to act first and think afterward when you felt that need to control?"

Rush shook his head.

Stridently, she shouted, "Never! I never did!"

Silence.

Ann walked back and forth in quick steps, turning sharply. "I nearly lost my life at the Wedge." She pointed at him. "You..."

"Ann, listen to me, please. How do I say I was a jerk and have you accept that. How..." His voice was loud and pleading.

She took three steps and stopped where her breasts were almost touching his chest. Her voice had a crackle like a bolt of lightning skittering across a darkened sky. "Goddamnit! What was it about you? We had such a good thing going, but on all this athletic crap you had such a terrible attitude. So you had a lousy childhood, you worked for everything you had, nobody ever gave you a break. That should round out your character, not turn you into a shit." Ann walked away, keeping her back to him.

"I..." He threw up his arms in a show of desperate surrender.

Turning, her voice unforgiving, "Do you see me acting like a privileged ass? Goddamnit! What was it about you?!"

No reply.

Ann's voice blared. Her anger at the months of inner turmoil Rush had caused spilled into her words. "I saved..."

The door to the conference room opened, "What's going on here? Oh, excuse me, Rush. I heard shouting and I didn't..."

77

"It's all right. Sorry if we disturbed anyone."

The deputy backed out as Ann picked up her briefcase and left.

JESSICA HELD Jonathan's hands. "We've talked so much about counseling. It's time. Nightmares are playing havoc with your health."

He slowly shook his head. "What can counseling accomplish? The worst is over. I have to work this out my own way."

"How will you do that? It's terrible what happened. Your nightmares frighten the children. They hear your screams in the dead of night."

"Give me a month or two more, please, I love you."

"But honey, this has been going on since the second conviction was reversed. What can possibly change you now?"

"Just a month or two more. If I'm not able to work it out, I'll go into counseling. Meanwhile, lets talk to Jeff again. He understands more and he's great with his brother and sister."

TEN

Investigator Dunley disliked Ortega Highway's winding, narrow route, especially on a hot day in an RV. Once he left the highway, it took another hour to take the correct dirt road and find the residence.

He looked around as he knocked on the door of the decaying house. In the side yard, two disabled cars were on blocks. Old and inoperable-looking pick-ups filled the dirt driveway. Empty beer cans so uniformly covered the front lawn they looked as if they had been planted there and were ready for harvesting. Trash blew about with every breeze. It appeared to be a graveyard for anything that man or nature didn't want. Curtains at the front of the house were dirty, torn, ill-fitting and hanging haphazardly.

The front door opened with a jolt, startling Dunley. "Wha da hell da ya wan?" The rough, gravelly voice matched the man. His full beard was unkept. The stained cowboy hat appeared welded to his head. A bulging, sloppy stomach leaked out between the buttons of his tight shirt. Khaki pants had a mixture of car grease, oil and innumerable food bits that had fled his mouth.

Dunley held out his identification. "Claudius van Towson?"

Towson eyed him with apparent suspicion, followed with a cruel, defiant laugh. "A cop? Alone? Here?"

Dunley pointed around him, his voice filled with sarcasm. "No asshole, ah got me a posse in them-thar hills." The comment silenced Towson even if it didn't frighten him. "You purchased a rebreather part from a dive shop in Dana Point."

Towson didn't open the cardboard-patched screen door. "Whazit ta ya?"

Diplomacy was out. "Would you like to drive to Santa Ana for our little talk?"

He looked at Dunley with apparent contempt as he grudgingly answered, "Yeah, I bought a part."

"Have you ever used a rebreather?"

"Hell no."

His attitude hasn't changed, thought Dunley, but at least he's answering my questions. "Where did you get the rebreather?"

"Motorcycle jamboree, north Arizona, las year. I won ut. Poker. Da Dana Point shop checked ut, tole me wha I needed."

"What's the former owner's name?"

"I dint get no names."

"What did you do with the part and the rebreather?"

"Fixed ut, run an ad, sole ut."

"Who bought it?"

"Shit iffn I know. A guy met me in San Juan Capo."

"Payment by check?"

"Cash. Two tousand green uns." Towson's mouth appeared to drool as he mentioned the sum.

"I assume you met him in some well-lighted area?"

"I know da ropes, I run wid a tough crowd."

"You met on a lighted street?"

"Yeah."

"Cars were going by, adding to the light?"

"Yeah."

"Describe him."

"Hey, I wuzn't dere fer luv." Mocking laughter.

Dunley's voice became more firm. "What did he look like? Or, would you like to go through three thousand mug shots, one by one."

"Asshole. Meedyum hite, meedyum bilt, meedyum-colored hair and skin, meedyum teeth, meedyum eyes, two hands, two feet, a hat and wearin glasses." Towson gave an ugly in-your-face laugh.

"When did you sell it to him?"

"Monts ago."

"Before June?"

Towson nodded.

Dunley looked at the man and his surroundings as he formed conclusions. Towson couldn't be the killer. He couldn't make it across the mouth of Newport Bay if he had a motor attached to him. A killer of Hermes' intelligence wouldn't have

Towson as a co-conspirator. Towson was just a loudmouthed motorcycle redneck.

He pulled out a business card and pushed it in through an opening in the screen. "Mr. Towson, I'll return. There are reasons why you should give me a better description. You're going to look at some tapes, too. Until then, I advise you to think long and hard about it, or you might be his next murder victim. Do you understand? The person who bought your rebreather is killing people."

Towson's mouth opened and made movements without sound.

Dunley laughed inside as he walked away. It'll make the next interview productive when we scare the hell out of him with telephone calls.

Towson slammed the door with such force the cardboard fell from the screen door.

Dunley turned. "Y'all come agin, ya' hear?"

"WHAT IS THE INDEX OF SUSPICION?" Rush asked.

Lieutenant Briden sat confident and relaxed. "It's the location of injuries which can help determine if a child had been intentionally beaten versus injuries from an accident. The index raises suspicion about the causes of injuries."

Briden laid a foundation for Briden's expertise even though Dr. Ben would be covering the same subject. Rush did this to give Briden credibility on other matters. "Please elaborate."

Briden faced the jury. "If a child falls forward, you'll expect injuries to the palms of the hands, elbows, knees, tip of the nose, forehead, chin, and so forth. Those are the prominent areas of the body that will first strike the surface."

"If he falls on his back, the prominent areas are the back of the head, shoulder blades, buttocks, calves, and so forth, the parts that stick out.

"Suspicion arises when injuries are to the non-prominent areas of the body. For example, either side of the nose, upper lip under the nose, inner portion of the upper arms, chest areas below the armpits, inside the thighs, back of the neck and the small of the back. Though there are exceptions, a falling child doesn't normally injure non-prominent areas.

"Also, it's necessary to look at the number of injuries a child may have in non-prominent areas and in totality. There may be so many the child would have to have fallen a great number of times. The severity of those injuries may have made multiple falls impossible because the child may have been rendered unconscious by the severity of the earlier falls.

"If the bruises are of varying colors, it shows they didn't occur at the same time. All such observations must be made to determine if child abuse existed."

Rush shifted his focus. "Did you see the defendant in Robbie's room?"

"Yes."

"Describe what you saw."

Briden described Tabbetts' indifferent and complacent attitude regarding Michelle and Robbie.

"What was the result of your search under the warrant?"

"We found no physical evidence that directly or indirectly tied the defendant to the child's injuries. Nor did we find anything that might have been an instrument used to inflict the injuries on Robbie."

"No further questions."

"Ms. Cavanaugh, cross?"

Ann saw multiple brush fires with this witness. She'd have to be patient and work it as specifically as she could. Briden was not a witness who could be intimidated, nor would he lie.

"Haven't you seen injuries on children in non-prominent areas that weren't caused by child abuse?"

"Yes."

"In other words, a child might fall on a toy that strikes the small of the back or under the nose on the upper lip?"

"Yes."

"Then the fact alone that injuries occur to the non-prominent areas is not proof of child abuse?"

"No, as I previously stated, you must look at the entire picture."

Ann didn't like the way Briden touched the jury. So what. Rush's medical experts will say the same thing. Move on. "Had you ever met Mr. Tabbetts before that morning?"

"No."

"Then you don't know how he reacts to serious injury to a family member or loss of a loved one?"

"I was talking about Mr. Tabbetts on that specific June morning."

Ann had again laid a specific foundation for a defense she'd delineate at a later time. "Did you look at Mr. Tabbetts' hands?"

"Yes, his knuckles weren't bruised, if that's your next question."

Ann smiled at his response. "Nothing further, Your Honor."

As Rush rose for redirect examination, the court-clerk's telephone rang. A brief conversation occurred, after which she scribbled a note for the judge.

Goldensmith turned to the jury. "Ladies and gentlemen, I must speak with the attorneys. Please remain seated. "Mr. Jones, Ms. Cavanaugh, please come to my chambers."

"Orange police called. Attorney Stephen Maldive was found dead in his car in the garage of his home. An apparent suicide." He handed the address to Rush. "I read the story about the attorney murders in this morning's Times. I'm sure you want to get right out there."

Goldensmith ordered the jury to return the next morning. Rush turned to Ann. "You're coming with me."

She appeared to resent the commanding tone of his voice, but turned to follow.

MY GOD, if I had called that press conference even one day sooner, if I had - if - if -" He repeatedly clenched his fists on the steering wheel. "Maldive would have taken precautions." He felt ill.

"You couldn't have done it any other way."

He reviewed the murder scenarios. "Hermes seems to plan everything around the routines of his victims." The guilt of Maldive's death returned. "Think! Hermes has seen the newspapers by now. He'll be angry, speed up his timetable as a show of bravado, and even resort to violence without trying to mask the deaths as suicide or accident."

They arrived at Maldive's home at three in the afternoon. As they walked into the garage, Detective Mary Mascotti, Orange police, glanced in surprise at Ann's presence. "It's OK," he volunteered, "she's the next victim."

Ann grimaced.

Mascotti gave a concise account. "The body was discovered about an hour ago by the gardener. He saw lights in the back of the house. The rear sliding door was open, the screen door closed. He thought Maldive had come home early but didn't see him around anywhere. When he finished his work he didn't want to leave the house like that. He yelled into the house and looked around the garden. He found Maldive in his car in the garage. The motor wasn't running. Out of fuel. Battery dead."

"And?"

"A section of the garden hose was used to pipe the exhaust into the car. We found the knife where the main hose was located."

"The key was in the ignition and turned on?"

"Yes."

"So, this probably happened last night. You're checking all that?"

"Right."

Dr. Ben joined them. "A plug nickel was under Maldive's tongue. It's like a piece of metal you'd punch out of an electrical box."

"The charade is over," Rush added in a somber tone.

Dr. Ben relayed more facts. "This death has all the earmarks of a suicide. If Maldive had imbibed too much, it would have made the killing simple with ether or chloroform. I don't think he'd use ether because it has to be constantly administered, especially if Maldive were sober. Hermes wouldn't have time for that. Both chemicals have a distinctive odor."

Mascotti asked, "What if Maldive actually committed suicide or cooperated with Hermes."

Rush's eyes widened. "Meaning?"

"About a week ago we had a 911 call. His housekeeper found him on the floor. Pills and liquor. There are previous incidents."

"Interesting. Send me copies of your files." As Mascotti nodded, Rush turned back to Dr. Ben. "What about chloroform?"

"I smelled around his clothing and face," said Dr. Ben. "Nothing. Of course, it depends on how much was used, evaporation, and other odors masking it. It's difficult to detect chloroform in the body as part of an autopsy, especially from what I'm seeing here. Incidentally, I got a whiff of an air freshener."

An officer at the door of the garage waved to Rush. "Judge Goldensmith's on the phone. Tabbetts' trial."

Motioning Ann to follow, he went to the house and picked up the phone. "Hello judge, this is Rush."

HERMES HAD EXITED I-55 on Chapman Ave., going east toward the hills surrounding Jamboree. Turning right onto Crawford Canyon Road, he drove the winding roads through the hills where three cities and county territory met. Depending on which turns he made after he had reached the restaurant at the top of the hill, he was either in sheriff's county territory or the cities of Santa Ana, Tustin or Orange. Maldive, a widower with no children, lived in Orange.

The curbside mailbox was a carved wooden miniature of the house, with a street number and Maldive's name. The garage stood separately, fifty feet off the street. Lots were large and homes were positioned to give owners privacy.

This killing would be a companion piece to the demise of Polperro, Horne and Baumholtzer. *I'm an artist, even though I'm destroying, not creating.* Hermes smiled, it showed he had great range.

He posted a letter at the main Orange post office.

LATER THAT NIGHT, he drove to a restaurant in the hills of Orange and parked his car. Removing a small briefcase from the trunk, he put it in a paper bag and walked down the hill to Chapman Avenue. Walking a mile west, he took a cab to a restaurant in the vicinity of The Bar.

Shortly before midnight he walked to The Bar's parking lot and waited in the shadows near Maldive's Lexus. Within forty-five minutes, Maldive exited, his gait unsteady. Hermes stepped out.

"Mr. Stephen Maldive?" He held out his hand as he came toward him. Maldive appeared hesitant. Hermes added, with a righteous flair, "Kurt Baumholtzer sent me!" He saw the expected shock on Maldive's face.

"Kurt? He's dead!"

"Oh, my God, no! I'm sorry, I didn't know."

"Electrocuted. Accident."

He observed Maldive's mushy speech. His brain was probably formulating the necessary words to carry on a conversation but the mouth couldn't coordinate fast enough to use all of them, selecting only the operative words.

Hermes expressed his sympathy, and added, "He spoke so highly of you."

"What? When? I don't understand?"

"I'm being accused of murder. I'm innocent." Maldive appeared fascinated. "Mr. Baumholtzer said I need you if I'm really innocent."

Again, he held out his hand. "My name is Stephen Philcrest." Maldive took it as Hermes continued. "Proud to know you, Sir. Mr. Baumholtzer said it was a blessing men like you were still gracing this earth."

"Call my office, at nine, appointment."

Hermes put on an expression of despair and hung his head, as he stammered. "The police have been at my house. Are you going home? May I drive with you? I can tell you about my case and take a cab back. I'm desperate. My children..."

"Kids?"

"Yes, Sir. Five. All under ten." He gently grabbed Maldive's shoulder. "Please, I'm innocent. Help my children! My family!"

He waited and looked around. There hadn't been any other people in the lot since they met. That couldn't last. If Maldive didn't cooperate, he'd have to subdue him, shove him in the car, drive away and kill him the old-fashioned way.

"Get in," said Maldive.

Hermes opened the front passenger door with a handkerchief in his hand, blocked his hand from view with his body as he sat in his seat, closed the door and put the handkerchief in his pocket. He took a quick look at the gas gauge. Enough. Thank Zeus for small favors.

Hermes briefly explained his fictitious case. A short time later they pulled into Maldive's garage. "Come. Drinks, talk." Hermes again used his handkerchief.

Maldive unlocked the back door, turned off the alarm system and laid his keys on a table. Entering the family room, Hermes sat in an arm chair while Maldive went to the bar in the far corner. Making scotch on the rocks for both of them, he handed a glass to his guest. Hermes brought the glass to his lips but didn't drink.

Hermes expertly answered Maldive's questions.

After a moment of silence, returning to his chair, Maldive said, "I'll take your case." Due to the hour, his age and the alcohol, he slumped to the side of his chair with his chin on his chest.

Hermes put on latex gloves and cleaned up the room. Turning off the lights, he drew Maldive forward, picked him up, soothed his mutterings with soft talk, carried him to the car and placed him in the driver's seat.

Returning to the house in darkness, he went to the kitchen, found a large serrated knife and Maldive's keys. He secured the cut garden hose from the exhaust pipe to the driver's window and sealed everything.

Wearing a chemical mask, he opened a can of chloroform and poured some on layers of terry cloth, which he pressed to Maldive's nostrils.

Using a damp cloth he wiped Maldive's face, placing the cloths in a plastic bag.

Stripping the gloves from his hands, he placed them in a plastic bag and put on another pair. Hermes straightened Maldive's clothing.

A slight spray of air freshener in the car and the garage dissipated the chloroform odor that hadn't already evaporated.

The plug nickel couldn't go between Maldive's false teeth so Hermes put it under the tongue. Hermes realized that with this death, Rush's lack of cooperation, and the newspaper story that would break later this morning, the charade of accident or suicide was over. He started the motor, exited, closed the door and returned to the garden. Going through a mental check list he was satisfied he had taken care of everything, including leaving a partial roll of tape that had been used to secure the hose to the car, and, placing Maldive's prints on everything pertinent to the suicide.

Returning to the house, he turned on the family room light and exited, leaving the sliding screen door closed but the French sliding door open.

Maldive was being transported. He would no longer be in any turmoil about the differences between justice and injustice.

At the peak of his career, Maldive was the top criminal defense attorney in the county. There is no statute of limitations on his sins, thought Hermes, pleased with what he had done. Sadly, he suspected, Rush wouldn't share his enthusiasm.

At the restaurant parking lot, Hermes got into his car and drove home.

ELEVEN

Hermes reached into a bag for an empty soup can from which he had cut out the bottom and top. He put m&m's in his mouth and dialed Maldive's home telephone number.

Maybe prosecutors were just lawyers with a changeable label. Prosecutors one day, defense attorneys the next, or even judges. It troubled him that there were no fine lines of distinction. "We're advocates, we can represent any side," they say. How can they do that, he thought, when each side demands a different mind-set. They're hired guns, pimps. Look at Ann Cavanaugh. Former prosecutor, now a criminal defense attorney. They don't change. Ann Cavanaugh. What a pleasure it'll be to kill her, especially for having the gall to defend a man like Tabbetts. Rush's *hello* interrupted his thoughts.

"*Click.* I'm really disappointed in you, Rush,...*click...click...* giving the newspapers the story. *Click. Click. Click.* Even though you disagree with me, *click...click...click...click...*this was our secret. *Click. Click.*"

Surprised, Rush remained calm but blunt. "You left a plug nickel in Maldive's mouth. Why a suicide look and then leave a calling card?"

"*Click. Click. Click.* Some things were our secret...*click... click...* Now, I don't...*click...click...click...*care. It doesn't matter...*click...*anymore." Successive *clicks* rattled out as he adjusted the candy in his mouth. "*Click.* You're just another shyster."

"We'll catch you, Hermes, make no mistake about that."

No reply.

"You respect me," Rush said, "or you wouldn't have written those letters."

"I'm not...*click...click...click...*interested in talking to you anymore. *Click. Click.*"

"I do understand your thinking and..."

"NO - YOU - DON'T! *click.*" Hermes shouted, feeling he was being toyed with, demeaning his intelligence.

* * *

"We can work this out." Rush couldn't help the urgency in his voice. He noted Hermes voice sounded metallic and hollow.

"Why did you call me...*click*...a nut? *Click.* Why...*click*...*click*...did you stoop so low? *Click. Click.* We had something going, you and I... *click*...*click*...*click*!!"

Build his ego. "It takes an extraordinarily organized, intelligent and disciplined person to make murders look like suicide or accident."

"Thank you. *Click.*" But it appeared to be a matter-of-fact reply.

"What's behind the plug nickel? I thought Charon wanted silver."

"The plug...*click*...*click*...nickel tells...*click*...Charon what lawyers are...*click*...*click*...*click*...worth."

Rush concluded Hermes believed he was part of the mythology. It was no longer an alter ego.

"Don't you see the...*click* ..*click*...irony in all this? The dead lawyers..*click*...would jump at the...*click*...chance to defend me. *Click. Click. Click. Click.* The public...*click*...interest, the challenge and publicity would...*click*...*click*...make them drool. *Click.*"

Rush sadly agreed with that reasoning. "Hermes, let's meet, talk, face to face. No tricks. Name the place and time. Any conditions."

No reply.

"Well?" Rush waited, hoping."

"*Click.* We've already met...*click.*"

The comment chilled Rush, piercing his reserve. He unsuccessfully tried to avoid verbalizing surprise. "What?! Wh..."

"...we've already met...*click*," he repeated.

Rush clenched his teeth to remain silent.

"*Click*...and, we've already...*click*...*click*...*click*...talked, face to face...*click.*"

Rush sat, stunned, unable to keep his usual poise.

"There's...*click*...nothing to...*click*...work out. *Click.* You're my enemy now...*click*...*click*...*click*...I hate lawyers...*click*... regardless of the label. Watch your back. *Click. Click.* You're on my list."

Rush briefed Ann, Dr. Ben and Mascotti on the call and asked Mascotti to inform the newspapers that Maldive's death was murder. "You'll do all the usual checks like talking with the neighbors, tracing Maldive's movements last night, and so forth?"

Mascotti nodded.

THE D.A.'S CONFERENCE room had a funereal atmosphere. Mascotti appeared lost in thought, Cortez and Hightower stared at the wall.

Kevin Dunley explained that hidden cameras had been positioned in the Tabbetts' courtroom to videotape everyone but the jury.

"We also checked out The Bar, since both Baumholtzer and Maldive had been there just prior to being murdered. Non-lawyer faces were seen around there the past couple of months, which isn't unusual, but nothing came of it. Credit card receipts developed no clues. Checking out the media for possible threats by victims or their families produced nothing.

"I have the courtroom video set to roll. Between us we either have photos of the rebreather owners in Orange County or we personally interviewed them."

Cortez added, "We should also look for people in disguises."

"An investigator was posted in the hallway outside the courtroom with a hidden camera," Dunley said. "Since the courtroom is at the end of the hall we don't get passers-by. Roll the tapes."

No identifications were made.

AS RUSH WALKED into his office he rethought his trial tactics on the Tabbetts' case. It was an ever changing scenario and he had to keep ahead of it. Michelle Tabbetts would name her husband as the one who had beaten Robbie. Medical expertise about the injuries would convince the jury Robbie had been murdered. Ann's cross-examination of Michelle would be brutal.

Concentration became difficult.

Putting on latex gloves, he found and opened a letter that had no return address. The text was obviously from the same typewriter as the first two. The letter "t" was slightly turned from its true vertical position and the top of the "t" wasn't fully printed.

He read the text.

> *It is the act of a coward to wish for death*
> *Seneca, Metamorphoses*

The message appeared apt. But how would Hermes know that? Maybe he didn't. Yet, Rush made a mental note to follow up on that thought. But how?

RUSH RELISHED the surprise he had prepared for Ann. Of his last three main witnesses, Ann would expect Michelle Tabbetts to be next on the stand, followed by the radiologist and then Dr. Ben. Chronologically, it made sense. But, it would allow Ann to use Michelle to change the thrust of the facts surrounding the x-rays before they even got into evidence.

Turning his back to the jury, he looked at Ann and said, "The People call Dr. Stanley Tetley."

Ann gave an abrupt move in Rush's direction but he gleefully turned away.

Dr. Tetley came forward. After being sworn and establishing his credentials, he stood at a lighted display where x-rays could be seen by the jury.

"Dr. Tetley, I show you six exhibits." He read their numbers aloud. "They are x-rays of Robbie Tabbetts taken in a hospital in Santa Fe, New Mexico, on February second of this year. Have you seen them before."

"Yes, a week ago."

"Looking at the rib x-rays, what do you see?"

"I see a total of six rib fractures. Two on the left and four on the right." He medically identified them. "The body mends broken bones by fusing them with calcium deposits. No such deposits exist on these photos."

"Are you able to tell whether they were broken on February second?"

"No, the deposits of mending calcium are not an exact science. It depends on the age of the person and other things. But, I can say the fractures shown on the February second photos had occurred in close proximity to that date."

Rush presented Tetley with the set of x-rays from Children's Hospital of Orange County, CHOC, and identified them for the record. "Dr. Tetley, have you seen these photos before?"

"Yes, I saw them on the morning Robbie Tabbetts was brought to CHOC."

"Please look at the photos of the ribs and tell the jury what you see."

He displayed them on the lighted exhibit stand. "I see the same six ribs I referred to in the Santa Fe photos. They now have calcium deposits where they had mended. Those ribs have been refractured."

A few of the jurors stifled apparent outrage.

"Do you see anything else?"

"Yes, there are two fresh, additional, rib fractures." He identified them. "This is in addition to the six ribs that I've already talked about. We now have eight fractures, two fresh and six refractures."

Tetley next reviewed and compared the photos of Robbie's skull taken on February second and those taken on the day of Robbie's death. "In my opinion, the February-second photos show a single fracture of the skull. It's difficult to determine if it is a fresh or recent fracture. Unlike fractures of the ribs, skull fractures fuse with little calcium."

"And what about the photos on the day of Robbie's death?"

"Those photos show the skull fracture I just referred to on the Santa Fe photos had been refractured and there are two new fractures of the skull. Three total."

"When a skull fracture fuses, is it as strong as it was before?"

"Yes."

"When fractured ribs fuse, would they be as strong as before?"

"Yes. And, I should note that the rib fractures are in an area that would take the blow from any frontal blunt force. If the same force were applied to those fractured ribs the second time around, it's expected they would refracture in the same area."

"Dr. Tetley, what can you tell us about the bones of children who are approximately twenty-two months old?"

"Their bones are soft and supple. A child of Robbie's age would have to be struck or hit with greater force than that applied to an adult to break that child's bones."

"No further questions."

Ann finalized her decisions as she rose to cross-examine Dr. Tetley. *I cannot dispute Dr. Tetley's opinions or that Robbie had been badly beaten. Target Michelle Tabbetts.*

"Dr. Tetley, were you in Santa Fe hospital when Michelle entered with Robbie?" Ann expected negative answers to her questions. It was merely a method of forcing the jury to think about Michelle Tabbetts instead of Dr. Tetley's testimony.

"I was not."

"You don't know if Michelle Tabbetts brought him in, whether she stayed with him or what she might have said while she was in the hospital?"

"I don't know that."

"In fact, you...'

"Objection, your Honor," Rush stated, "Dr. Tetley has stated he wasn't there. There's no foundation for him to answer."

"Sustained."

Ann coughed to make sure the jury would probably look her way. She smiled, as if indicating she had touched a raw nerve and the prosecution was trying to keep her from cutting deeper. "No further questions." *That's playing the game.*

"**WHAT WOULD HAPPEN** to my finger if I put it in a live socket?" Detective Hightower, in the office of consulting engineer Bill Petrus, had generally explained the basis of his inquiry.

"Electrical burn, depending on how long you touched the circuit."

"What if a live wire was laid across my palm?"

"You'd have an electrical burn that conformed to what touched you, a line-shaped burn."

"Assume my palm had a large red area. Nothing charred, nothing burned. Could electricity cause that?"

Bill softly whistled. "Electricity can be diffused, spread out, so to speak. One moment." He returned with a sheet of copper. "If I put one hundred and twenty volts in contact with it, your skin would turn red when you laid your palm on it. Depending on how long you held it there, and other factors, the palm wouldn't be charred or burned in the way that touching a live wire would cause."

The direction of the answers elated Hightower. "But if it's still one hundred and twenty volts, why doesn't it leave the skin charred or burn me just like a one hundred and twenty volt live wire would?"

"Look at what the person is touching." He pointed to the plate. "Maybe this will explain it. If you put water in a tall test tube, the water would have depth. Put that same water on a large dinner plate, it spreads out."

Hightower's eyes widened. "The electricity in the copper plate spreads out!"

"Right, like the water on the dinner plate, it diffuses."

"But could it still kill?"

"Oh yes. It's still one hundred and twenty volts. It just kills you without burning you like a live wire would."

TWELVE

Michelle Tabbetts wore minimal make-up and, with confidence and poise, took the stand.

"Mrs. Tabbetts," Rush began, "you're the birth mother of Robbie Tabbetts?"

A quiet, firm reply. "Yes."

"Your husband is the defendant?" He pointed to him.

She turned from the jury and looked at the defendant. "Yes."

"How long have you been married?"

"Fifteen years."

"Is this your only marriage?"

"Yes."

"And your husband's only marriage?"

"Yes."

"Was Robbie the only child of your marriage to the defendant?"

"Yes."

"During your marriage, how many times were you pregnant?"

In a strong and clear voice, "I had five pregnancies prior to Robbie's birth and all ended in miscarriages."

"Did you want children in your marriage?"

"Yes."

"Did your husband want children in your marriage?"

She hesitated. Her mouth tightened and her voice faltered. She shook her head. "He said he did, but Robbie's death has convinced me otherwise."

Rush shifted the scene to keep the jury alert. "Were you and the defendant in Santa Fe on February second?"

"Yes, we arrived there about a week before that date. It was to be a vacation and skiing trip."

"Did you and the defendant go skiing while you were in Santa Fe?"

"Once for me. He was out about five times."

"Did you want to ski more?"

"I did." Michelle's voice appeared to lose its assurance, and sounded troubled. "But I was confused."

"Would you please explain?"

"About one month prior to Santa Fe, I had noticed bruises on Robbie."

"Where were those bruises located?"

She didn't cry, but the jury appeared to hold her pain as she relived the memory. "On the chest, back, upper thighs."

"Were any inside the upper arm or on the sides of the chest under the armpits?"

"Oh yes."

"Inside the thighs and on the small of the back?"

"Yes."

"Did you know the significance of the locations of those bruises at that time?"

"No." Her lips quivered.

"Did you do anything as a result of your observations of the bruises?"

"I asked my husband but he had no information."

"Did he say or do anything indicating he was as concerned about the injuries as you were?"

"No. He merely said the kid was clumsy."

"Defendant called him *kid*, not *Robbie*?"

"Yes, he never used Robbie's name."

"Was Carmen Gonzales with you in Santa Fe?"

"No. My husband didn't want non-family on our trips."

"Did you talk to Carmen about the bruises before you went to Santa Fe?"

"Carmen was the one who brought them to my attention. My husband was not home much when Robbie was awake. I'm home enough that if Carmen had struck Robbie I would have heard him cry out."

That, Rush felt, deals a blow to Ann's case in trying to pin the injuries on the maid. She wasn't in Santa Fe in February, she couldn't have been responsible for those rib and skull injuries. Now it's between the two Tabbetts.

"When did you first discuss Robbie's bruises with your husband?"

97

"I spoke to him when Carmen first brought them to my attention and again on February 1, the day before Robbie was taken to the Santa Fe hospital, and subsequently."

"On February 1, did you show him the bruises before you spoke to him about them?"

"Yes."

"What did he say?"

"When I first asked the question, he appeared annoyed. I pressed the issue and he said the kid was clumsy."

"Had you ever personally witnessed Robbie falling or being clumsy in a way that would cause injuries?"

"Never."

On further questioning, Michelle related she finally went skiing on February first. Thomas stayed at the house. She got home after dark and went right to bed. The next morning she found Robbie unconscious and rushed him to the hospital. Her husband didn't appear at the hospital when Robbie was discharged because he had returned to Orange County on a business emergency. Robbie and she left Santa Fe the day he was discharged..

When the doctors told her of the skull fracture and broken ribs, they accepted the explanation her husband had given her. Robbie had fallen off the swings at the playground and had hit and bounced off a metal pole. Thomas Tabbetts didn't think it was a serious fall until he saw Robbie's condition the next day.

Rush wondered why the doctors treating Robbie in Santa Fe hadn't been suspicious enough to call the police. At least to have the parents questioned more thoroughly. He had experienced a few doctors not wanting to be involved in anything as a witness because it interfered with their practice and income. A little suspicion on their part and Robbie would probably be alive today.

He thought of another aspect of child abuse. Reading newspapers and listening to television news, it would appear that child abuse occurred only in the lower classes, the poor. Surely, intelligent and financially well-off people commit child abuse. But where are the complaints, revelations by the media? They keep it within the family, unless it becomes part of a heated divorce. The upper class advantage of money and position allows them to work around possible criminal charges. *You're in trial. Get back to business.*

"When you came home from Santa Fe, and up to the day of Robbie's death, did you continue to notice new bruises on Robbie?"

"Yes. I asked Carmen about them on many occasions and she said…"

"Objection, asks for hearsay."

"Sustained."

"Did you question the defendant about the injuries?"

"He appeared indifferent, with no attempt to discover the problem, even blamed Carmen. We got into arguments over his attitude. He repeated that the kid was clumsy."

"How was your relationship with the defendant during the period of February to early June?"

"Rocky. He'd work late, wouldn't join me on my social and charitable affairs, wouldn't spend time with Robbie."

Michelle went on to state she wanted at least five children but the defendant began hinting he wanted her all to himself and he didn't want anything else distracting him from his business.

"The night before Robbie's death, what time did you leave the house?"

"Early evening, possibly around seven."

"You didn't put Robbie to bed?"

"I got him ready for bed. My husband put him to bed."

"Did Robbie have any bruises that evening?"

"Yes, numerous ones of different colors. But he was alert and active."

"Whenever you were with Robbie in Carmen's presence did you notice how he reacted to Carmen?"

"Robbie would hold out his arms to have her hold him. He'd jump between us."

"When you arrived home from Santa Fe, did you notice any reaction by Robbie when the defendant was near?"

"Robbie would cringe. If Thomas tried to pick him up, he'd kick and scream as though he were afraid."

"Was Carmen Gonzales home on the evening before Robbie's death?"

"No. She got the night off, leaving at five that evening. My husband and I were alone with Robbie."

"Did you have an appointment that night?"

"Yes, chairing an informal meeting of various charities, then some of us were going to socialize, dinner, drinks, and so forth."

"Did you want the defendant to go with you?"

"Yes, but he refused. I had a sitter ready."

Rush had no choice but to ask, "What time did you get home from your night out?"

"About four-thirty the next morning."

Rush didn't question Michelle further about her social and charitable schedule and how it impacted her family life. The less Michelle spoke the less chance of her contradicting herself on cross-examination. Ann would have to go into certain matters even though Rush hadn't covered them, giving Michelle the opportunity to be fresh and original. The case depended on Michelle's credibility.

Rush's next decision was a gamble. He would not ask Michelle whether Robbie was her husband's child or whether she had kept that fact from him. If Ann went into it it'd look as though Rush tried to hide it from the jury. That could hurt the prosecution's case. On the other hand, if Ann raised it and Michelle gave a reasonable hurtful-wife explanation, it could hurt the defendant's case and bolster Michelle's position.

If Ann doesn't question Michelle about Robbie's biological father, Ann will put the defendant on the stand, allowing the jury to hear the facts from the betrayed husband. It was a gamble. Many things in trial were like rolling dice, even betting against an opponent's roll.

"No further questions, Your Honor."

Ann's cross-examination of Michelle had to be like probing with a sharp scalpel in quick and certain movements. The jury was sympathizing with the mother and any attempts to cut her up had to be definitive and successful or the jury would dislike Ann and take it out on the defendant.

She also picked up on Rush's gamble about the biological father. It didn't surprise her. If she asked the question, Michelle's answer would give her a chance to explain that aspect of their marriage and diminish the fact she had committed adultery. It might even make the jury sympathetic to Michelle because of her five miscarriages and the defendant's attitude regarding Robbie. Ann decided to wait until her client took the stand. The defendant's explanation would look like Rush tried to cover it up and Rush may then have to put Michelle on in rebuttal. Ann could then attack her just before deliberations.

"Mrs. Tabbetts, the night before Robbie was taken to CHOC, you were out socializing until five a.m."

"Yes."

"How many hours, in an average week in the last year, have you spent in your charity work?"

Michelle thought for a moment. "About forty to fifty hours a week, with more than half of that time at or from my home."

"Mrs. Tabbetts, you saw bruises on Robbie a short time before going to Santa Fe?"

"Correct."

"Did you make any inquiries to anyone about those injuries?"

"I asked Carmen Gonzalez. She didn't know." Michelle explained Carmen Gonzalez's fifteen-year good reputation and background and then focused on the defendant in completing her answer. "My husband said he knew nothing about the injuries."

Ann gritted her teeth at Michelle's reply.

"The only explanation my husband ever gave me was that the kid was clumsy. And, of course, the fall off the swing in Santa Fe."

"Did Mr. Tabbetts spend as much time taking care of Robbie as you did?"

"No."

"Did he ever show a reluctance to be in Robbie's presence, to tend to him or otherwise babysit him?"

"No. But it was mechanical. He never showed emotion toward Robbie. Never did he just step in and do something."

"Did you ever see him treating Robbie in an objectionable manner?"

"No."

"In February in Santa Fe and in Santa Ana in June, when Robbie was unconscious, you took him to the hospital. Between those times, when you saw injuries on Robbie, did you ask a doctor for an opinion about whether Robbie was being beaten?"

"No." She lowered her head. "The serious injuries occurred only twice, February and June. Between that time there were just bruises. In June, it was too late. Robbie was dead. It was stupid and naive of me not to think of the criminal ways in which Robbie could have been injured. I've lived a sheltered life and just never thought people did such things."

"Last February, in Santa Fe, did you inquire of the doctors whether Robbie had been beaten as opposed to having suffered injuries from falling?"

"No. I merely told them what my husband had said."

"Did you ever try to get Robbie to indicate to you or tell you who, if anyone, was hitting him?"

"No. No. Stupidly, I did not. It was beyond me to even think that an adult would do that to a child or that a child Robbie's age could understand such a question and truthfully express himself on such an issue. I'll never forgive myself." She uncontrollably shook. The judge asked if she'd like a recess. Michelle shook her head. "Please, let's continue."

The display of emotion hurt Ann's case. She had to overcome its effect on the jury. "You said that after the February injuries Robbie would cringe or scream if the defendant came near him. Didn't that tell you something?"

"It should have. It didn't. There were times when I sensed Carmen wanted to accuse my husband but she probably felt it wasn't her place."

Ann sought a quick closure on her testimony. She would later reinvent Michelle's answers as her own guilt.

"Were you aware that when the medics and police were at your home last June, Carmen Gonzalez was about eight houses away and walking toward your home?"

Michelle appeared to lose her composure as her hands went to her mouth. "No - no, I was, I was, no - no, I wasn't."

Ann glanced at Rush, who appeared having difficulty maintaining his composure. However strong that evidence might appear to cause suspicion of Carmen Gonzalez, Ann knew the jury would discount it because Carmen hadn't been in Santa Fe with the Tabbetts last February, nor was she with Robbie the June night the injuries had been inflicted. However, it raised questions, and juries often hung or came in not guilty based on collateral evidence.

"Are you aware a neighbor spoke with her about the medics and police at the house?"

"No - no - who -" Michelle looked at Rush, apparently wanting an explanation. Her face appeared drawn and tired and her head slumped forward.

"Were you aware Carmen immediately left the area, never letting you or the police know she was there or where she could be reached?"

"No, I wasn't..." She slowly shook her head.

"No further questions, your Honor." Ann felt she had raised enough questions concerning Michelle's credibility.

"**THE DIRECT CAUSE** of Robbie's death was a ruptured spleen from a heavy blow administered to the body at the location of that organ." Dr. Ben had examined over four hundred cases of physically and or sexually abused children, twenty of whom had died from the abuse.

"You've visited Robbie's bedroom?"

"Yes."

"Describe the floor on the day of Robbie's death."

"A thick, plush carpeting over a dense pad on a raised hardwood floor."

"Could the spleen have been ruptured by Robbie's falling out of the crib?"

"Impossible. Not even if he had fallen on a toy. Not enough height to the crib and the floor was soft and flexible."

"Tell the jury what your examination and autopsy showed."

"I can describe Robbie's multiple injuries in only one way. It looked as though several people had taken turns punching him until they were exhausted."

"What were the ages of the bruising?"

"Anywhere from one day, which was most of them, to about two weeks. I determined this by the coloring patterns going from red, through various color phases of healing, to yellow. Of course, the color sequence will occur only if the person is alive.

"Most of the injuries were fresh and to non-prominent areas. Robbie would had to have fallen at least twenty to thirty times, on a hard surface, to sustain all those injuries. But he would have been unconsciousness long before he could have fallen out of the crib that many times.

"If he unintentionally fell out of the crib, would he climb back in just so he could keep falling out? That scenario fits nothing in my experience. On the other hand, if he intentionally climbed and fell out, why would he climb back in? Especially if he kept injuring himself? He accomplished what he wanted - getting out - so he'd stay out. Therefore, no more falls."

"Dr. Ben, did other observations aid in your conclusion that Robbie had been assaulted?"

"His spine was broken between the fourth and fifth vertebra."

"Was there anything unusual about that?"

"No external blunt-force trauma existed at that area."

"What does that mean?"

"If external blunt-force trauma existed at that area it would explain the damage to the spine. Without that trauma, I can only conclude that Robbie's back had to have been arched in such an extreme manner it caused the spine to fracture. It's much like bending a twig until it snaps."

"What else did you observe during the autopsy?"

"The back of the eyes, the optic nerve sheath, had bled. This indicates shaking syndrome. Retinal bleeding existed without intracranial hemorrhaging."

"What is your opinion of the cause of Robbie's death?"

"He had been badly beaten and shaken. All of it contributed to his death. The ruptured spleen was the specific and direct cause."

"Could Robbie's injuries have been inflicted by a man or woman?" Rush wanted to take as many issues away from Ann as he could.

"Most definitely. The child was young, offering no resistance."

"No further questions."

Ann had no questions. Her medical expert would agree with Dr. Ben.

Court recessed for the day.

WHEN HE LEFT the stand, Dr. Ben handed two reports to Rush. "Maldive died from carbon monoxide poisoning and he was drunk. But for the plug nickel under the tongue, forensics would show it as a suicide. Horne's forensics show death by asphyxiation."

"Any marks on the teeth? How good is it as evidence?"

"A dental expert said the striations on Polperro, Horne and Baumholtzer's teeth are not common at that location, they're consistent with forcing in a hard object. It's an up and down pattern and there's ever-so-slight chips at the bottom of the striations."

"The plug nickel in Maldive's mouth supports the theory a hard object was forced between the teeth of the others." Rush sighed.

"Hermes feels you've abandoned him. It's no longer a game."

THEY WALKED UP behind him as he unlocked his car. Something cold and hard pressed against his head. Spinning around, the gun barrel bit into his forehead. "No! No! Don't!" he shouted.

105

They laughed, eyes furtive.

"No! No! Don't"

He felt the barrel move to his left temple. Laughter. The heat and force of the discharge expanded the hole made by the bullet. Explosion debris discolored the wound area. No more pleas, no more hope. Dead.

With a giddy laughter, one of the two men kicked the body. Each then pumped three bullets into the victim's face, substantially obliterating it.

911 calls from bystanders. Identification and pursuit of the car within twenty minutes of the killing. Capture within another half-hour. No powder residue on the hands. A search of the chase route and the car located neither guns nor gloves. No defendant statements.

Breathing heavily, sweating profusely, Jonathan awoke without screams or terror. As he slowly gained recognition of his surrounding, Jessica was sitting up in bed, watching him.

"I thought it best to let you see the nightmare through. It went on for some time and you weren't thrashing and screaming."

He slumped over, laying his head in her lap. "All these years. Am I finally accepting what happened to Phillip? I'll never be able to forgive the killers or the system that remains so indolent and unaccountable."

THIRTEEN

Making first contact pleased Broxton because Rushton Fowler may be uncooperative, even offensive. Better that Rush didn't personally bear the brunt of a rejection.

The stately Fowler mansion could be seen from miles away. Outbuildings of equal quality were scattered some distance from the mansion, like errant children who had to have their own space.

He drove to the arched gateway and announced his presence at the telephone built into the wall. A straight one-mile road looked like a tether anchoring the mansion. A cowboy appeared and took him to the door, where they were met by a butler wearing tails. Broxton felt he had stepped into the 1800's estate of an Englishman in the American west.

The butler took him to a wing with an extensive library, comfortable-looking western furniture and animal trophies. The visual sophistication of the room made Broxton think the owner would talk and listen.

"Sir, Mr. Rushton Fowler will be with you shortly."

When the doors automatically opened a half-hour later, Broxton saw an old, sharp-faced man. He had assumed Rush's father would be about sixty. This man looked frail and older, yet he pushed his wheelchair with vigor, abruptly stopping short of striking Broxton. Rushton Fowler pointed to a chair, Broxton sat and the wheelchair was rolled within arm's distance. A chessboard, with pieces showing a game in progress, sat on a nearby table.

Rushton Fowler's lips were cracked and spotted. His hair appeared hastily combed, with face and hands well scrubbed. A western shirt, sleeves rolled to the elbows, had a liberal sprinkling of mother-of-pearl buttons. Remnants of knees were protruding against the pants like dagger tips, in contrast to the shoulders and arms that appeared to have sucked up the strength of the lower body.

The voice was more brusque and strong than what the body appeared capable of producing. "Don't waste my time with talk about blood ties. What does my son want?"

Broxton hadn't expected a paternity acknowledgment without prior conversation and documentation. Quickly reassessing the situation, he related Rush's background, and added, "Your son wants a father." There were no questions or comments. "I won't tell you more unless you're interested."

"Interested in what?"

Broxton was surprised at the off-handed way in which the question was asked. "In meeting your son. Establishing a father-son relationship." He wished his reply had been more forceful.

"Why isn't he here?"

Fowler's voice remained calm and gently inquisitive, but Broxton thought he had detected some pain or remorse in the question. "Your son thought you may want your privacy. If you didn't want to establish a relationship it'd be best you never met. His presence might have appeared to be a challenge, intimidation or threat. He doesn't know why he was abandoned, why you hadn't claimed him at birth, why you didn't attempt to find him during his childhood, why he was the one who had to hire a private investigator." Broxton glanced to his left and drew the baron's attention to the chess game as he added, "Your son has made all the correct moves and yet he feels he's the one in checkmate. He wants a father. It's your play."

"Does he want my money?"

"He wants the love of a father and mother, a bank account is not a condition." Broxton spoke strongly without pandering, pleading or groveling, but noticed the baron wince when *mother* was mentioned.

Fowler whirled his wheelchair and headed for the door. Just as suddenly he stopped and returned to Broxton. His spotted lips quivered, eyes became moist, and the voice strained with a combination of anger and inquiry. "Look at me! Look at me! Goddamnit, take a good look. It's too late for me to be a father! I can't...I can't..." The muscles in his forearms stood out as he gripped the wheelchair arms, knuckles turning white. It was as though he were asking Broxton to say that none of that mattered, that a father was a father with or without a wheelchair.

Broxton, deeply moved, felt distance and objectivity were the only way to confront Fowler at this moment. The baron was probably torn by more than the thoughts of his current physical condition. Many responses crossed Broxton's mind. He couldn't settle on any of them. He didn't know whether to pity him or ask to cast the past aside and act on what was left. Broxton couldn't estimate the time that passed as they silently confronted each other.

"Why don't you meet with him? It'll answer all your questions, all your doubts." Broxton took a gamble with his next comment. "It will give back much of what's been missing in both your lives."

Glaring angrily at Broxton, he wheeled around again and pushed hard for the doors. "The butler will show you out."

Broxton shouted, "Where can I find your son's mother!"

The wheelchair stopped, the baron's head drooped, but he didn't turn around. Moments later the butler came to the baron's side.

Broxton shouted across the room. "Mr. Fowler, think about this. Do you intend to also miss the rest of your son's life? You may have little time on this earth, but don't deprive your son of the memories of friendship and love in the many years he has yet to live. Don't deprive him of a future because of your past."

The baron disappeared into the far side of the large entry hall.

The butler showed Broxton to the door, stepped outside and spoke quickly. "Sir, I've been with the family for fifty years. Mr. Fowler is a fine gentleman. Don't think harshly of him."

"I understand his emotions. I want the best for both of them."

"Mr. Fowler wanted to marry Miss Jones. His parents threatened to disown him because of her background. He was the only son and felt he had to stay. This estate has tradition. Three years after Miss Jones left he was paralyzed when thrown from a horse. His parents died when their private plane `crashed four years later." The butler motioned to the cowboy to get Broxton's car.

"What about Peggy Sue Jones? Had he ever contacted her? Does he know where I can find her? Do you..."

"She died not long after his parents were killed."

"Died? Broxton did some quick calculations. "She would have been about twenty-six! "Where did she die? What caused her death?"

"Drug overdose, I'm sorry to say, Sir, in Texas. He felt his rejecting her caused the problems."

"How did that information get to him?"

"Miss Jones had only Mr. Fowler's name and address in her possessions. He took charge. Rightly or wrongly, he felt he cared more for her than anyone else."

"Where is she buried?"

"We scattered her ashes on the range where young Rushton was conceived. Mr. Fowler has left instructions to have his ashes scattered at the same place. He's suffered the misery of his decision every day since he rejected Miss Jones."

Broxton shook his head at the fears that prompted such a similarity of feelings in both father and son. "They both fear rejection." Broxton's car arrived. He shook the butler's hand and thanked him. "I'd like to propose something."

"Sir?"

"I'm going to have young Rushton come here unannounced. Would you admit him to the great room and then bring in Mr. Fowler?"

"Yes, Sir, I would. I may be risking a great deal but it would be a positive thing to do." He made a slight bow and went into the house.

Broxton reprimanded himself. During his investigation in Montana never had he thought Rush's mother would return here, dead or alive. He should have checked, inquired, and had that information for Rush on their previous meeting. Live and learn.

"**I WISH IT** had come out differently." Rush sighed as he digested what Broxton had told him of the meeting with the baron.

"Underneath all the posturing he's hurting as much as you. I think he feels you'd reject him because of his physical disabilities and frailty. I know you'll do the right thing."

Rush's voice flowed with confidence. "It has to be more final than where he left it. We need each other."

"I knew you'd see it that way."

"**MR. TABBETTS,** please take the stand."

Ann wanted to keep her direct examination brief. "Did you want children in your marriage with Michelle."

As he continued to do throughout his time on the stand, Tabbetts turned to the jury when he answered a question. "I wanted children badly so I could leave my stock brokerage business to them. Except for Michelle, I have no family."

"Weren't you concerned about Michelle's health after five miscarriages?"

"Very much so. After the second, I suggested we adopt."

"Did she agree?"

"No."

"Did she say why?"

"Yes, she said she wanted the child to be biologically ours. Prior to marriage we had agreed to have a large family. I had been alone for many years, building my business. Marriage entails children."

"Do you know the cause of her miscarriages?" This could entail hearsay evidence but there was a point where Rush would not object for fear of making the jury think he was trying to hide something.

"Her activities aggravated internal problems that made it difficult to carry a child to full term. She was to spend at least the last four months of her pregnancy in the house, resting. Despite the medical advice she continued her full schedule of activities."

"Are you the biological father of Robbie?"

"I am not."

The jury audibly murmured. Ann marked certain DNA documents, and had the defendant testify to his part in obtaining the DNA results, intending to call expert witnesses at a later time.

"Did your wife ever tell you you were not the biological father?"

"Not until I confronted her shortly after Robbie's death."

"Have you ever beaten, hit, angrily touched or caused any physical injury to your son, intentionally or otherwise?"

"Never." He shook his head.

"Have you ever seen Carmen strike Robbie?"

"Yes, the first time was just before we went to Santa Fe in February."

"Where was Michelle?"

"She was standing next to Carmen."

"Did Michelle try to stop or reprimand Carmen?"

"No."

"Did you do anything?"

Tabbetts lowered his head, as if in pain, defeat and self-anger. "No."

"Why not?"

"I loved Michelle. I was afraid of losing her."

"Even against the possible loss of your son?"

"I never expected it to go that far." He squeezed shut his eyes for a moment, opened them and continued. "I guess I blocked it out." His fists clenched and tears came without sobbing or verbal grief.

"When Michelle left the house the night before Robbie's death, did you check on him before you went to bed?"

"Yes. I looked in on Robbie about ten that night. I could hear his breathing. He rolled over and stretched."

"What is the current status of your marriage?"

"I filed for divorce the day after Robbie died."

Ann saw the positive effect of that statement on the jury. She had convinced Tabbetts it would be a great tactical move. Another law firm was handling the divorce so it wouldn't appear Ann had orchestrated it.

"There's evidence you were not grieving for Robbie. In fact, you were portrayed as having been antagonistic to the efforts of the authorities. Do you have any explanation?"

Tabbetts sighed. He appeared to use his public relations acumen to great advantage. Ann had told him to be self-deprecating in certain instances. Admitting mistakes and appearing human is something juries eat up.

"I can readily see where they would have honestly concluded I was cold and antagonistic. When I was ten years old, my father, mother, five-year old sister and two-year old brother were killed in a traffic accident near our home. I saw my baby brother's body at the scene. Last June, in Robbie's bedroom, I thought I was ten again, looking at my brother's body. It was as if I had never grown up. My mother and father, sister and brother were gone. I felt trapped, as if my life had come full circle and I'd have to live the nightmare a second time. I..." Tabbetts shook his head.

Ann waited until she had wrung the last drop of sympathy out of Tabbetts' performance.

The prosecution heard this evidence for the first time but the judge wouldn't allow a recess in the trial so the facts could be investigated. He told Rush he could attack it another way.

"No further questions, Your Honor."

"So," Rush asked, "Michelle didn't want children but you did, so you could pass your business on to them?"

"Yes."

"How old were you when you got married?

"About forty-three."

"Why didn't you get married earlier?"

"Too busy."

"Wouldn't you expect your wife to raise the children, leaving you to run your business?"

Tabbetts hesitated. "I guess so."

"While you were single, weren't you seeing women and having sexual intercourse?"

"Objection, your Honor! Irrelevant!"

"Your Honor," Rush quickly interjected, "it goes to one of the defense issues."

"Overruled."

"Yes, I was having sex with women prior to my marriage."

"Couldn't you just as easily have gotten married during those years, had your children and fulfilled your wishes regarding a family?"

"Perhaps, but I was very busy then."

"Mr. Tabbetts, "Isn't it true you were out of town for a two week period just prior to the date of Robbie's birth?"

"Yes."

"And, isn't it true your appointment books show you've been working an average of sixty hours a week since Robbie was born?"

"Yes."

"Then tell the jury, Mr. Tabbetts, how your present work schedule differs from the times before you were married?"

"It didn't really differ, but when I was single, I didn't have to go home when I was finished working."

"Since your work life hasn't changed, you could just as easily have gotten married thirty years ago and had your children at a much younger age?"

"I guess so."

"How old are you?"

"I'll be fifty-eight this year."

"And Robbie would have been two this year?"

"Yes."

"You'd want Robbie to get a college education, hopefully a law degree or an MBA or both?"

"Yes."

"That means Robbie would have only summers to learn your business and he'd be about twenty-six or so when he finished his graduate degrees. That would put you at age eighty-two when he began work full time."

"That sounds about right."

"For a man who wants a son or daughter to take over his business, doesn't that give the impression time wasn't of the essence?"

He shrugged. "It's what I had to contend with."

"Isn't it true you didn't want children?"

The defendant came defiantly erect in his chair. "No, that's not true!"

"Did you know a Maria Hullbert and a Constance Phillips?"

Tabbetts, appearing worried, glanced at Ann. "Yes."

"Weren't they past lovers, prior to your marriage?"

"Yes."

"Your Honor," Ann quietly said as she rose, "this line of questioning is irrelevant to the charges in this case and we have no evidence from the prosecution regarding this issue."

Attorneys were called to the bench. "Mr. Jones?"

"Your Honor, the defendant has raised the issue he wanted children and his wife did not. The prosecution will show that just the reverse is true."

"Your Honor," Ann replied, "the prosecution hasn't shown this evidence to us."

"The records were delivered to me just before the defendant took the stand. This is my first opportunity to present them to Ms. Cavanaugh." He explained what evidence he had and the applicability of it.

The judge turned to Ann. "I'll call a short recess. Look over the evidence and tell me if you're going to have an objection. Unless you can tell me the prosecution's documents are not accurate and you have evidence in that regard, the trial will continue. You'll have time to talk to your client."

Ann reviewed the files, spoke with Tabbetts and made the appropriate objections. All were overruled.

Rush picked up two files and approached Tabbetts. "Weren't both women carrying your baby at one point in your relationships?"

"Yes."

"There were a total of three pregnancies and you paid for three abortions on fetuses that had no medical problems?"

Tabbetts faltered. "Yes."

"But for the abortions, you'd now have children who'd be about eighteen to twenty-one years old!?"

"Yes."

115

On the issue of Tabbetts' demeanor on the day of Robbie's death, Rush questioned why the defendant hadn't produced official records of the death of his family so the jury would have documents regarding the truth of his statements. Tabbetts said the county where his family died couldn't find the records.

Rush turned to take his seat at the counsel table. Keeping his hands close to his vest he formed a circle with the index finger and thumb of his left hand and held his right index finger in the circle. Ann saw the sign from the moment he held it while looking at her. She reluctantly smiled.

"No further questions."

Court recessed for the day.

"HOW'S THE SURVEILLANCE at your home?" asked Rush.

"There's little privacy, but I can't complain."

"You don't have to stay in the house, Ann. There'll be enough movement with lights going on and off. Hermes will assume you're home."

"You really believe he could come after me any time?"

"Yes. It could be a bullet through a window, nothing sophisticated - just kill."

She nodded, held out her hand and forlornly said, "I appreciate your concern."

He held it firmly and laughed. "When I realized you'd be on Hermes list, it was a tough struggle with my conscience to tell you."

She smiled, appreciating the joke and how it fit into their relationship.

He released her hand. "Joe Broxton talked to my father yesterday, would you like to hear about it?"

Ann smiled. "Yes, I would," and agreed to having coffee.

He told her everything he had learned and showed her his birth certificate, saying, "My life's been validated."

They small-talked and Rush's pulse quickened. Perhaps she was seeing a change in him. Finally, Ann picked up her briefcase to leave. "Are you going to Montana?"

"As soon as this trial is over and we clear up the major leads on the Hermes case. I figure about three weeks."

"Good, you should go."

FOURTEEN

Ann lived in Turtle Rock, an exclusive area of Irvine. A six-foot high slump stone wall sealed off the large yard of her home from the side street, from the neighbors to the back, and on the other side. As she drove up the hill to her home, she decided to hire a contractor to build a fence around the front and install electric gates. Aside from Hermes, her profession made her the target of kooks.

She had asked Rush to move in with her three years before they broke up. "It'll be more convenient than spending half the nights at each other's place."

They swam, biked, ran and took vacations together to compete in triathlons. He was a gentleman, kind and helpful, all the things she wanted in a relationship, except for his compulsion to control.

Then came the incident which Rush couldn't forget nor admit his error in judgment. It caused a major change in him. He couldn't accept the double blow to his ego, being wrong and facing the near-disaster he had caused. She told him he'd have to leave. The only person who had gotten her mind off Rush was Polperro, and to this day she wasn't sure if her feeling for him had been genuine.

Ann saw the unmarked police vans. One parked across the street from the front of her house and the other on the side street at the rear of her yard. She parked at the end of the circular driveway. Exterior house lights were off. If Hermes was to make an attempt to kill Ann, the police didn't want to frighten him off by making the house look unapproachable. Drapes and shutters were closed, but interior light could be seen from the street. Inside, Ann greeted Detective Hightower. "Where are the other officers?"

"Officer Smith is hidden in the rear shrubbery, next to the neighbors' fences. He'll be able to observe if anyone attempts entry from other yards. Officer Pearce is in the kitchen at the rear of the house. Each van has a two-person team, everyone has night vision goggles and headphones to minimize communication sounds."

"Sounds good." She went into the kitchen, fixed dinner and retired to the den to work on Tabbetts' case. At ten she went to her bedroom, took a handgun from her briefcase and laid it on a bedside table.

MASCOTTI checked the time. Eleven-thirty at night. A car reached the top of the hill and slowed in front of Ann's house. Over secure net, she quietly said, "This is Mascotti. A car is going into the driveway, headlights on, barely moving. Passing and parking in front of Ann's car, facing the street. I can't get the plate number because of the angles. Lights and motor still on. Someone's getting out. My God!"

Hightower stood inside behind the front door. "What's going on?"

"Somebody dressed in a clown suit! Baggy clothes, bulbous nose, floppy shoes, big clump of fuzzy hair! Like Ronald! The clown is going up the steps...stopping...looking around..."

Mascotti's narrative was interrupted by Cortez's whispering voice from van two on the side street. "Hightower, someone in dark clothing scaled the wall from the street..."

Officer Smith, in the yard shrubbery, interrupted Cortez. "Man...dark clothing...yard."

Pearce, in the kitchen, added, "I see him."

Hightower warned Ann about the visitors and instructed her to get on the floor. Ann grabbed her handgun and did as requested.

Puzzled, he returned to the living room. "This doesn't fit, but we'll play them both as killers and partners. Mascotti, leave the van and get as close as you can to the clown. Your partner stays put, keeps us informed, phone for silent back-up and call Rush to get here immediately. Cortez, position yourself outside the wall, your partner can watch your back and any possible escape by the suspect in the yard. Smith, stay where you are and report only if Pearce misses something. Move only to keep the suspect in sight. We have to let him enter the house. Pearce, you will do all the communications on the suspect in the yard."

119

The doorbell shattered Hightower's concentration on the rear-yard suspect. He removed his headset. The light in the entry hall remained off. Taking his handgun from his shoulder holster, he held it behind his right thigh as he opened the door.

The clown's bulbous nose lit up and blinked. He smiled and reached into a pocket in the oversized pants. "I have something for Ms. Cavanaugh."

Mascotti leaped from behind the clown and clamped an arm around his neck, smothering his mouth with a cloth wrapped around her hand. Hightower's gun pressed hard against the clown's head as they noiselessly pulled him inside the house, closed the door, thrust him to the floor and handcuffed him. Mascotti showed the clown her police badge, kept her handgun at his head, and motioned him to stay quiet.

Hightower hurriedly holstered his handgun and picked up his headset. "We have the clown in custody. Report."

Officer Pearce whispered, "Suspect is at the outside rear. Checking family room window...rear door...kitchen window...all locked."

Hightower replied, "I'm joining you."

Pearce pointed to the kitchen window as Hightower crawled into the room. Hightower kept everyone informed. "Suspect at kitchen window."

Suspect covered much of the glass with tape, followed by a blunt sound. Glass shards fell to the counter, followed by the steady noise of someone clearing the glass in the area of the window lock.

Reaching inside, suspect opened the lock and pushed up the bottom window. He moved one hand around the counter as if checking for breakables. Apparently satisfied, he climbed in.

Hightower and Pearce watched with their flashlights ready. Pearce held a gun. Hightower tapped Pearce on the arm. Both beams struck the masked suspect as Hightower shouted, "Freeze!"

Suspect made a quick move for the window but Hightower wrestled him to the floor, securing him with handcuffs.

*   *   *

"Have they been questioned?" Rush asked as he came running into the house.

"No, this is your show," said Hightower.

"Let's talk to the clown. Has he been searched for weapons?"

"Yes. None."

Ann joined them as they walked to the front of the house. The clown sat in a chair, hands cuffed behind him. Rush nodded a hello to the other officers, removed the cloth from over the clown's mouth, and pulled up a chair to face him.

The bulbous nose and wig had been removed. His eyes appeared to be exploding in bewilderment. The odor from the clown's pants, and the wet spot on the floor where the clown had been lying, verified his fright. With a thin face and slight build, he appeared to be in his mid-fifties.

Rush took a slow, deep breath. "I'm going to remove the cuffs. Would you like something to drink?"

He shook his head and rubbed his wrists.

"You've been informed you're in police custody." Rush kept his voice low and well modulated, wanting to relax the suspect, as he went through the formality of the Miranda rights. Suspect waived and agreed to talk. "What's your name?"

He tried to speak.

"Take your time. Swallow, relax, no one's going to hurt you."

After a series of swallows that diminished in rapidity, he mumbled "Aubrey Simpson."

"Good. Thanks for your cooperation. Now, why did you come here?"

His voice gained composure. "I - I was to deliver a birthday gift to a Ms. Cavanaugh, and - and - do a dance routine."

"At this time of night?"

"It's - it's our specialty. Odd-ball hours, odd-ball performances. My wife works for the Odd-Ball Greetings Company." He twitched a little. "They handle the off-beat situa - situa - situations. I'm a tech - computer - by day but I do things - I do things - like this at night for extra income." His

121

gaze turned from the floor. "I'll never do this again." He looked at the mess on the floor as he moved uncomfortably in his seat.

"Where's the gift?"

The clown looked at Mascotti. She took a brightly packaged, thin, five-inch square item from the table next to her. "This was the only thing on him, except for his wallet. His I.D. backs up the name."

He held the package up to the clown's face. "Is this it?"

"Yes."

"The dance routine, was it anything special?"

"Special?"

"Yes, special. Does it have words with the steps? Is it from a musical? Does it have an ethnic theme?"

"It's Greek."

Rush's face strained as he glanced at Ann. "Why weren't you wearing a Greek costume?"

"Somebody else had it." He shrugged, as if wondering what the big deal was about a clown doing a Greek dance.

"Do you know what the present is?"

The clown's head shook.

"Did the person who ordered this gig wrap the present?"

"I don't know."

Rush gingerly felt the package, not concerned with lifting prints. Hermes would have been as careful with the package as he had been with the letters. It didn't appear to be any heavier than what the weight of the paper and ribbon would be. His fingers worked in from the outer edges and confirmed the contents.

He handed it to Ann. "Here, birthday girl, it's for you."

Ann slipped the ribbon and unwrapped it. The plug nickel startled her. Rush took it.

Rush asked the clown. "Did the dance have any words?"

"No, I quickly went over a few steps I remembered from *Zorba the Greek.* I expected to hum the music."

"Did you have a letter for her or were you supposed to tell her something?"

"Well, yes. That's what was really strange."

Rush waited.

"After I finished the dance, I was to hand her the gift and say *Evil events from evil causes spring. Aristophanes.*"

"Mr. Simpson, I believe you're not involved with what we're investigating, but we'd like your cooperation. Call you wife, tell her you're here and you're returning with the police. An officer can get on the phone to reassure her. We need to possibly learn the identity of the person who ordered this birthday wish." The odor caused Rush to add, "Go into the bathroom and clean up, an officer will accompany you."

Rush, accompanied by officers and Ann, went to the rear of the house. "If the burglar is Hermes, he used the clown as a feint to get Ann to the front door so he'd know what part of the house she was in."

"He had a loaded thirty-eight handgun, no ID and no extra ammo," Hightower explained.

The suspect, wearing black, was lying face down on the kitchen floor, a black watch cap next to him.

Rush kneeled and rolled the suspect to his back. An Anglo, athletically built, clean shaven and about thirty.

The suspect spoke first. "What the hell's going on? You couldn't know I was going to do this."

Rush informed the suspect of his Miranda rights and the charges, including four counts of murder.

The suspect swallowed rapidly as Rush recited the charges. His body stiffened but he refused to answer Miranda questions. Rush waited.

Suspect broke the silence. "What's this murder crap?"

"You know, Hermes." Rush waited for a reaction to the name.

"Hermans? My name isn't Hermans!"

Rush tried to imagine it with a mouth full of m&m's. "What's your name?"

Silence.

"You've got to have a record. We'll know who you are within hours. You've been caught red-handed on a residential burglary, possessing a loaded gun. I'm sure this isn't your first felony. The three-strikes' law will nail you. With murder, I'm going for the death penalty."

"Who are you?"

"Rush Jones, criminal prosecutor, I'll be handling your case."

"Thanks, I always like to know who I'm talking to. Mr. Rush Jones, go fuck yourself!" He rolled over on his stomach.

Rush turned to Hightower. "Run his background. Get search warrants of his car, house - whatever we can locate."

In the living room, Rush paced back and forth. "I have a bad feeling."

"I know," responded Mascotti, "the clown was too obvious. The burglar seems like a pro and capable of murdering people, but I get the feeling he has nothing to do with Hermes."

"Hermes wouldn't have a partner. Ann, what do you think?"

"I think the clown was sent by Hermes. It's a million-to-one shot the burglar picked this house at the time the clown arrived. But what other explanation is there?"

"So why send in the clowns - if you'll forgive the expression - if Hermes didn't act on it?" Cortez wrinkled his forehead.

Rush thought for a moment and blurted, "That's it! Hermes *is* acting on it. The clown was a feint to throw us off his true intentions. If Ann had been home alone when the clown appeared she would have called 911 immediately. Hermes wanted us to concentrate on her. Call Thomas Tabbetts and Goldensmith and put them on alert." He pointed to Hightower, "Notify Santa Ana PD and Anaheim PD and get officers to their homes immediately! We'll wait here until we hear from them." He looked at his watch as he added, "This was a diversion." He slammed his fist on the table. "Damnit! I said he'd change his routine!"

Ann took the phone from her ear. "No one is answering at Tabbetts' house."

Hightower lowered his cell phone. "Goldensmith has been alerted."

FIFTEEN

HERMES HAD DRIVEN by Ann's residence with the commuter traffic earlier that evening. The two maxi-vans were plain, not the fully-equipped party or camping vans residents in this upscale neighborhood would own. "The cops are here, they think Cavanaugh is next. Zeus, you're really looking after me."

Later that night he went north on Flower Street, east on River Drive in Santa Ana and parked at the end of the block, on the other side of Flower from Tabbetts' house.

It took three minutes to get to Tabbetts' front door. He pressed a button and lit up his watch. The clown should be arriving at Ann's house. The doorbell rang loudly. A shuffling noise came from inside.

"Who is it?"

"Herman Wilcox," Hermes softly said, "I'm one of Ann Cavanaugh's investigators. The District Attorney has some potent new evidence and we have to talk about it before court tomorrow."

"How do I know you're who you say you are?"

"I'll hold my identification to the peephole." Exterior light came on.

Tabbetts looked through the peephole. He saw a middle-aged man wearing a shirt, coat, tie, hat and aviator glasses. A thick moustache appeared to cover much of his lower face. Something about him looked familiar but he couldn't place it. "I can't read it."

"I can give you Ann's private home number or hand you my identification. Take your pick." It was taking a chance Tabbetts would make the decision that would allow him to enter the house. No choice. He had to put Tabbetts at ease.

No response.

"Mr. Tabbetts, are you still there? Please, do something or tell me how to handle this. Ann is waiting."

The knob turned, the door opened and stopped when the chain lock reached its limit. Hermes quickly looked at the street, kicked the door with the flat of his foot, and barged in.

125

Tabbetts was sprawled on the floor, trying to get up. Hermes closed the door and repeatedly kicked Tabbetts.

Tabbetts moaned and appeared dazed. Hermes grabbed the neck of his robe and dragged him to Robbie's room. Throwing Tabbetts onto the carpeting, he turned a wall lamp to low and again kicked him.

Hermes selected a baseball bat from a large trunk filled with toys and athletic equipment. Tabbetts sat up. He shoved the bat under Tabbetts' chin, lifted his head and stated, "You killed an innocent child?"

Tabbetts sucked in his cheeks and his eyes kept shifting over the room as he spit out a tooth. Without looking at Hermes, he mumbled, "Maid, wife, not me."

"Undress!"

"What?"

"Undress! Everything! Stay on the floor!"

Tabbetts undressed.

Hermes took two steps forward. "This is for Robbie." The bat struck Tabbetts across the shoulder and chest, knocking him flat.

Tabbetts curled into a fetal position, crying with pain. "Money? Do you want me to say I did it? What do you want? I'll go to court. I'll confess, what do you want me to do?"

"You miserable baby-killing creep!" He raised the bat over his head.

"I'm innocent," looking Hermes in the eye and spitting blood, "until proven guilty…right to defense…lawyer…jury."

Hermes' face tightened, his mouth went dry. "Right to a defense? A lawyer? Jury of your peers? Presumed innocent? I'm your judge, jury and executioner. You're all presumed guilty. You, your lawyer, the whole stinking system."

In swift motions, Hermes took off his hat, fake moustache, glasses and wiped the cosmetics from his scar.

Tabbetts eyes appeared to bulge and he moaned, "You? You! What…why…why are you…?" as the bat struck him on the head.

Hermes swiftly did a tattoo over Tabbetts' body. When he was satisfied he had fractured the skull a number of times,

126

broken all the ribs and ruptured the spleen, he checked the pulse. Dead - or as good as.

Lifting the body into the crib, he arranged it in a fetal position. "May Charon feed your bones to the dogs that guard his world. May Hades make your soul know everlasting agony."

He forced a plug nickel between two of Tabbett's upper front teeth. The telephone rang. Hermes wanted to pick it up. Rush had probably figured out what had happened.

Hermes gently closed the front door and headed for his car as he listened for sirens and looked for flashing lights. Reaching Flower, he paused long enough to feel secure, and sprinted to his car. As he heard police cars coming north on Flower, he drove away, sticking to side streets until he reached Main Street.

"**WE KNOCKED** on the front and back doors and on several windows. No one answered. No inside noises. Closer inspection showed a slight splintering at the edging of the front double doors, about where a chain lock might be. We forced our way in." Briden hurriedly explained what they had done as he motioned them to follow.

An envelope, addressed to Rush, was taped to Tabbetts body in the crib.

Rush's stomach churned. "Have you taken a video?"

Briden nodded.

Rush donned plastic gloves and saw the plug nickel embedded between the teeth. Opening the envelope, he read the contents aloud.

> *Law is a pledge that the citizens of a state*
> *will do justice to one another.*
> Aristotle, *Politics.*

The telephone rang and Rush quickly said, "It's for me," as he turned on his pocket tape recorder. His voice had a raw, firm, intolerant edge. "Well, you nut, you're no better than the man you just killed."

Hermes voice showed anger as he shouted. "*Click.* You've never...*click*...understood! *Click. Click.* You don't see... *click*...the evil...*click*...in the justice system. You haven't... *click*...seen people you love,...*click*...*click*...destroyed, with little or no retribution. *Click. Click. Click.*"

Rush heard the same hollow, metallic voice as on the previous call. His mind flirted with the reason. *He said we had met, talked. It had to have been sometime between the Baumholtzer and Maldive deaths because that's when he added the new sound."*

"What did killing Tabbetts do for you? He isn't a criminal lawyer."

A shrill and angry reply. "*Click.* I just got...*click*...tired of seeing...*click*...*click*...the same old defense *click*...*click*... *click*...crap. Juries often buy that. *Click. Click.* Tabbetts was ...*click*...*click*...an appetizer, lawyers are my main dish, my... *click*...sacred mission!"

"It's a sacred mission and you're killing them?"

"All the gods kill. *Click. Click.* Don't you read history? *Click. Click.* Religion...*click*...has been the biggest...*click*... *click*...purveyor of death...*click*...*click*...*click*...in the world."

"I guess I don't get it, Hermes. You're supposed to be this Greek god, following mythology, yet, you send me quotations from Seneca. There's enough famous Greek literature to tell you how screwed up you are but you must think ignorance is bliss. You're just a simple-minded killer acting out of frustration. You're not a Greek god."

"The quotations...*click*...*click*...fit the occasions...*click*."

"You've made a mistake, Hermes." Rush sounded like a drill sergeant. "You let me in on your plans, thinking I'd help you in some way."

A minute passed, followed by a second hesitant response. "*Click.* A-And?"

"Now you can't let go. You need me, Hermes, I'm your conscience. I'm telling you you're wrong and you don't like that."

"*Click. Click.* Rush?" The deliberate voice sounded hurt. They had broken whatever bonds they may have had left.

"*Click. Click. Click.* Someone has to...*click*...fix the system. *Click.* Justice is delayed,...*click*...thwarted, twisted,...*click*... denied, laughed at...*click*."

Rush's fatigue showed in his angry, dismissive voice. "So you're the cure?"

Hermes' response sounded calm and resolute, without animosity, as though he wanted to make a simple point between parting friends. "Don't try to kid me. *Click. Click.* Don't kid yourself. *Click.* Every man's ethics has its vulnerable time...*click*...*click.* You just...*click*...haven't come across yours yet. *Click.*"

Rush squirmed. He had had his vulnerable times. His mind reflected on some moments of anger and frustration, but a clear line separated him from Hermes.

"The next time...*click*...we're in personal contact...*click*... you will die. *Click. Click.* I will not...*click..click...click*...call you again."

AT ANN'S HOUSE, police checked the interior and exterior and informed Ann their one-week surveillance was the maximum their department's budget could handle. They advised her to get private security guards. Rush, checking his handgun, volunteered to stay at the house until daylight.

Ann told Rush he could take the guest bedroom next to hers.

Rush talked about Hermes' comment of having met and talked with him, stated all the things his secretary and he had done from his appointment book to discover when or how he might have met Hermes. Forty males in Tabbetts' jury pool were an impossible task, but they worked through it. "How frightened are you?" asked Rush.

"I'm not as scared as I thought I'd be."

Rush frowned. "That's difficult to understand."

"Hermes won't try to kill me like he killed the other lawyers, and he won't be as violent as he was with Tabbetts."

"Why not? He's lost it! I don't understand you."

"Follow this. I'm a woman. I think he'll want to toy with me to my face. He'll wax philosophical and make me the verbal brunt of his anger with the criminal justice system. He thinks he's a superior masculine type. He doesn't see much danger in me one-on-one. I'm just a *girl*."

Rush felt exasperated. "And that's why you're not frightened?"

"All I'm saying is that not having to fear a shot in the dark or a knife to my back does make a difference."

"Honest to God, Ann, you actually feel you have a chance if he confronts you face to face and has a chat with you?"

"I'm saying I'm more mature and equally intelligent. Physically? that depends on the situation." Ann appeared to formulate her feelings in a way he'd fully understand. "I don't like being prey for the foreseeable future. If I'm right in how Hermes will approach me, perhaps I can reverse our roles."

Rush's exhaustion prevented him from grasping the intent of Ann's last comments. "It's past three in the morning, but there's something I need to finish."

"Our interrupted conversation in your conference room?"

"Yes. You did something good for me at the Wedge, Ann."

"Good? What an odd word for saving your life. I've done a great many good things for you during our relationship. Why don't you tell me every moment of that Wedge scene? Does it hurt that bad?" Without mocking, she added, "Acknowledge your mistakes."

Rush hesitated.

Ann took the offensive. "I back-pedaled on a wave that wasn't breaking properly but you decided to go for it. I saw you were in trouble. The wave broadsided you down." The memory of it appeared to change her. Her erect posture faded.

Rush rose and took a few steps toward her but she backed off.

"I went straight to the bottom, searching for you, taking a million-to-one chance on the direction the current would be dragging you. I splayed out my arms and legs trying to cover as much area as I could, just hoping to hook onto you, grab you, do something to find you and bring you up."

Rush sat, burying his head in his hands, recalling his stupidity.

"Do you know how close I came to letting you go because I couldn't hang onto you and save myself too? I thought I was going to die because of your bravado, your foolishness. Do you know how that felt? The medics spent more time on me than on you! I nearly died, and, unlike you, I wanted to survive!"

He raised his head, managing only a whispered reply. "I'm apologizing from the bottom of my heart. I was wrong. I've changed. I'm asking you to give me another chance."

Ann showed fatigue. "I didn't want to be thanked or owed. I just wanted our life to go on without any more of your athletic machismo crap." Tears moistened her face.

Rush stood and held out his arms.

She rose and backed away. "But you got worse. You couldn't take the mistake you made compounded by the fact that you would have been responsible for my death. You ranged from sullen to antagonistic. You couldn't swallow your pride, admit your error, and change. I finally told you to move out." Ann, crying, ran to her bedroom.

IN THE HALLWAY, after the judge dismissed the Tabbetts' jury, Ann turned to Rush. "Thanks for your help regarding Hermes."

He reached for her hand. She let him take it. "It's my job, but it's personal too." Ann smiled as he continued. "I'm stuck on telling you things that are giving me closure." He took a deep breath. "When all this is over and you're out of danger I'd like to date you again. You can check me out to see if I've really changed."

"It might be worth a try, but if I see any of the old Rush in you it won't take more than a millisecond for a permanent *sayonara*." The blunt comment matched her unsmiling face.

He swallowed. "So what are you doing for the rest of the weekend?"

"I've got a full schedule." She saw the disappointment in his eyes.

Nick Novick

JESSICA AWOKE and found Jonathan, fully dressed, sitting in a large armchair in a corner of the dimly-lighted bedroom. Two o'clock in the morning. "Is anything wrong? Why aren't you in bed?"

"It's just nice to sit here, Jessica, look at the bed and know I don't have the usual fear of going to sleep. I feel I'm going to be OK."

Jessica went to him and sat on his lap, hugging him as he tightly held her. "I'm so happy to hear that. I admire your strength and resolve. Was it just time that enabled you to do that? Meditation? What? The problem seemed insurmountable."

He carried Jessica to the bed, set her down, and sat on the edge of the bed. "I worked through the problem. I'm just intent on doing positive things. Tonight, I feel especially comfortable. A little more time and this'll all be behind us."

He put an arm around her waist and drew her to him as she passionately kissed him.

SIXTEEN

"Hello."

"Mrs. van Towson, is Mr. van Towson in?"

"N-no. Who - who's callin? Is - is - this you agin?"

"It's me again, the rebreather buyer. Now look, I don't like being danced around. I want to see him and talk."

"H-he ah-h-h, he's away, won't be back fer a week."

"Did you tell him about my calls?"

"Yeah, but he dint say nuthin'."

"That's it." Rush's tone remained hard, sinister, and abrupt. "Talk to the cops and he's a dead man." He hung up, satisfied that after three previous calls the groundwork had been laid for Claude van Towson's cooperation.

RUSH AND DUNLEY drove north on Main Street to gain entrance to the I-5 going south.

Dunley filled Rush in on the investigation. "We've checked out the alibis of all the rebreather owners in the county. They're clean, including Sullivan and Briden."

"So Claudius van Towson is our last hope."

"We've been checking his place but he's never around. His wife was told we're cops checking out some murders. She's pressured."

They parked within a quarter mile of Towson's house. Until midnight, each took turns staying under cover and approaching the house, hoping to spot Towson.

ANN TOSSED IN BED, trying to get comfortable. The clown and burglar at her house, Tabbetts' death, dismissal of the Tabbetts' jury and then that sensitive conversation with Rush, had made it a long night. She wondered if the apparent change in Rush would be permanent. The clock struck twelve noon.

She dressed and drove to the grassy area on Ocean Avenue, above Corona del Mar State Beach, across the street from Polperro's home.

Looking at the blue Pacific, she made her decision to sail to Santa Catalina Island. Being only Thursday, it'd be a long weekend. *Can I really handle this?* Her triathlon experience didn't give her the temperament to play a waiting game as prey.

Driving her Mercedes sports car, she picked up the phone and told her office manager to clear her calendar into next week. In less than forty-five minutes she was boarding her thirty-four foot Swan at Dana Point Marina.

A sailing checklist revealed no problems. With the engine running at five knots, she cleared the marina and unfurled the mainsail and jib. The wind puffed them out like the tops of freshly-baked muffins. A headwind demanded tacking. Her mind felt as though it were clearing.

Ann arrived in Avalon Bay close to five hours later, tied her boat to a mooring and took the dinghy to shore. Entering the Busy Bee Cafe, she took a table on the outdoor patio overlooking the water. It had been a favorite place of theirs when Rush and she were lovers. The serenity of Catalina Island compared somewhat to some of her favorite places in Europe, though she wasn't kidding herself. This isn't Europe. Look at the wealth, the lack of European culture and atmosphere. But for something that was just twenty miles across the water from home, the island and the Busy Bee Cafe offered something unique: an outdoor patio, the sea, and hills.

Ann concentrated on her Blue Lagoon drink, but found it difficult to exclude Hermes from her thoughts. Hermes. Hermes. *Had he followed me?* Many scenarios went through her mind as she tried to conceive the ways their meeting would begin and what her reaction would be. *He won't look at me as a strong physical opponent.* She got angry. *Damn him, he thinks he can toy with me because I'm a woman.* Noticing her shaking hands, she wondered if she were setting up her own death.

LATE FRIDAY EVENING Dunley stood behind a tree, watching. Towson came over a knoll from the south, toward the back of the house. He moved cautiously, taking cover whenever possible. Towson entered the house. Dunley called Rush.

Checking their handguns, Rush set the plan. "Take the rear of the house. Stand off a way so you can see him if he exits through a side window. I'll go to the front to establish contact."

They kept to cover as much as possible. Dunley sprinted for the rear position while Rush raced to the front door.

He knocked loudly and the door rattled in its ill-fitting frame, magnifying the sound. No one answered. He pushed out a piece of cardboard covering a hole in the glass, cupped his hands to his mouth and shouted, "Towson, come here!" Heavy footsteps appeared to speed up and then fade.

Rush whirled, taking cover behind an abandoned pickup truck. Hearing the back door slam, he looked to the rear of the house. The running figure had to be Towson. Rush ran in pursuit. Dunley left his cover, took out his handgun and stood in Towson's path.

"Stop!" Dunley shouted.

Dunley shifted his gun to his left hand. Towson, who had no weapon in his hands, appeared intent on running over him. Dunley kept his position, nimbly sidestepped and gave a hard jab into Towson's ample gut. He went down, groveling in pain. Dunley holstered his handgun as Rush reached his side.

Twenty minutes passed before Towson showed signs of communicating. He held his stomach and whimpered, "Don't kill me, don't kill me! I dint say nuthin. Lemme talk ta da guy dat sent ya!"

Dunley grabbed Towson and lifted him to his feet. "How do we know you're telling the truth?"

Towson's face showed fear. "The cops er calling er cumin by all da time. I said nothin."

Rush went nose to nose. "We're the cops." They showed their identifications and Towson appeared to recognize Dunley. "Five men have been murdered. You may be the answer, but you're acting more like the problem."

Towson's face appeared to brighten. "Cops? Yer not..."

"What are you talking about? What happened?"

He spoke rapidly, as if it'd give him more protection. "Yestiday me wife got nother call from da guy who bought me rebreather. He wanted ta talk ta me and said I wuz dead iffn I squealed."

"Where are your wife and kids?"

He motioned with his head. "Dat way, wid friends."

"You're dealing with a mad-dog killer. The guy who bought your rebreather used it to drown his first victim. You're the only person who can identify him." Rush paused to press a finger into Towson's chest. "He wants you dead!"

Towson began to tremble. "Wats da diff iffn he kills me now er later?"

"If you identify him, he'll only get out of prison in a box."

Towson didn't reply.

Rush was impatient. "You don't have much choice. If we don't catch him you're a dead man. If it happens around your family, they're dead too. We have some video tapes in an RV up the road. You're going to look at them under strict rules. Follow?"

Towson grimaced.

"I need to make a call. Meanwhile, you think about it."

He nodded.

"Hi, what do you have?"

Hightower responded, "The clown's legit. I interviewed the clerk who took the order for Ann's house." Hightower's voice deflated. "He turned out to be one of those rapper types on a summer job from high school. You know, the kind that keeps saying 'cool, cool, cool,' to everything you say but doesn't listen to a word?"

"So what happened?"

"Mr. Cool didn't follow most of the procedures for a night greeting, like photocopying the purchaser's driver's license, and so forth. They take those precautions because some people try to use their services to annoy people they don't like."

"Did you get any help out of him?"

"He said the suspect dressed in loose clothing, wearing a baseball hat, aviator sunglasses and had a moustache.

136

Useless description. Paid in cash. No car seen. It's a dead end. No prints. Suspect wore gloves, stating he had a skin infection."

"And the burglar?"

We made him on prints. Twelve-page rap sheet, mostly residential burglaries. He was in custody for possession of cocaine over the time of Baumholtzer's death. He talked to clear himself on the murders."

Rush's voice showed fatigue and disappointment. "Thanks. You've all done a great job. I'll be in touch."

"Let's go, Towson. And don't - I warn you - don't give me a hard time. If the killer got to you I wouldn't feel you were an innocent victim."

They settled in the RV. Dunley instructed Towson. "Look to see if you know anyone in these videos. If you think you can identify someone, just tell us without pointing. We'll instruct you from there. Claudius, look at me."

Towson looked and scowled. "Claudius, we may have to repeat each video a hundred times to be sure you had a chance to look at all the faces. We're going to freeze-frame whenever we come to a large group. You're going to have to look at each face. Until you satisfy us you're conscientious about what you're doing, you won't be finished."

FRIDAY EVENING Ann arrived at the Busy Bee Cafe and took a table at the isolated back end of the wooden patio, behind the restaurant building. The late afternoon sun watercolored the bay in splashes of orange, green and blue as the boats gently bobbed. To her back was a large plexiglass that separated Armstrong's Seafood restaurant patio from the Busy Bee. The only people who could spoil her quiet time would be those who sat at the table next to hers.

She pulled out her current read, a book of historical events titled *March of Folly*, by Barbara Tuchman. Ann's bookmark was a picture postcard of Walter's Wiggles on the trail to Angel's Landing in Zion National Park. She had hiked that trail with Rush a number of times and never tired of the scenery.

A rich, formal-sounding voice, politely interrupted.

"Ms. Cavanaugh?" Ann raised her head. "Yes, it is you, Ms. Cavanaugh. Hello. I was number four on your Tabbetts' jury. Jonathan Kent." He held out his hand.

RUSH TURNED on a recorder and laid a foundation of who was present, time, date, location and what they were doing. They went through three days of videotapes taken inside the courtroom. Towson, without success, followed instructions on five reruns. Dunley ejected the last courtroom tape and showed those taken in the hallway.

During the second showing, Rush noticed something in Towson's body language which appeared to indicate he may have recognized someone. Rush said nothing. He wanted Towson to initiate the identification, but he made a mental note to observe Towson closely when that segment was shown again.

On the third run, Rush tried not to show his fatigue. "Well, anything so far?" He again observed Towson's body language as he leaned closer to the screen. Rush grew tense as he calmly said, "You see something?"

"I - I - cant b'sure. I don't wanna finger da wrong dude."

"We don't want you to. We'll do this by the book."

Towson spoke to Dunley. "Reverse da tape fer ah few secs an freeze." Dunley followed the instructions. Towson pointed to a group of faces on the film and added, "Git dem full face fore dey turn inta da courtroom. Freeze as ya go. I wanna follow da faces from da side."

Dunley was asked to do it again and again. Towson nodded toward the TV screen. "I tink I see da guy."

Rush held his breath to keep from springing forward and shaking the information out of Towson. The identification had to be rock-solid. "Let's first cover a few matters. I understand your rebreather buyer was wearing a hat, glasses and had a moustache when you met him on a lighted street at night."

Towson nodded.

"Speak up, we're recording." Rush repeated his statement.

"Yeah."

"Why do you think you can make an identification under those facts?"

"Da lip fuzz wuz fake. It wuz one ah doz bushy ones and it dint fit da face. Moustache wuz dark, sideburns blond. Glasses wernt sunglasses. Dey dint hide much. Der wuz sumtin bout his head shape and face. It wuz...he...he...seemed pretty."

Dunley and Rush said nothing.

Towson continued. "He haggled price. We wuz dere 'bout twenty minutes. The longer we wuz dere the better I seen. Cars wuz lightin up da face."

"What was it about his pretty face?"

"He wuz pretty - handsome, not like me biker friends. His face reminded me ah doz people ah seen in mags at the docs."

"What magazines?"

"National Geo something, statues, people, way back when."

"Like way back when?" Rush bit his tongue to keep from hinting.

"Like - like Greek er Romin?" He didn't sound sure of his history.

Rush felt better about the basis for the identification. "Why didn't you just tell us that when Dunley was first here?"

Towson assumed his belligerent self. "Ah don't like cops. Iffn it wuznt fer me wife and kids ah'd tell ya ta go ta hell."

The answer pleased Rush. "Ready to make identification?"

"Yeah."

Rush remained patient. Once the choice was made the case could go speedily forward to an arrest. If the choice was wrong - but Rush didn't want to think about it. "You're not just shining us on?"

Towson replied with emphatic belligerence. "Ah don't give shit bout ya." Then he nodded toward Dunley as he rubbed his gut. "Er him."

"Point to the person who bought your rebreather."

Towson leaned forward. His finger touched a face before they could see his selection. As he withdrew his finger, Dunley and Rush looked at each other, unable to speak. When the shock of the identification left them, their words were a whispered but desperate duet. "Jonathan Kent, Tabbetts' juror number four!"

SEVENTEEN

Introducing himself, Jonathan Kent held out his hand. Ann remained calm, but found it difficult to respond. For some reason, the chance meeting with a Tabbetts' juror jarred her. Recovering without abruptness or surprise, she put the marker in her book and closed it. Smiling, she rose and shook Kent's hand. "Yes, of course I remember you. What are you doing in Catalina?"

"I'm playing catch-up on my business appointments."

"I remember you have a family. Are they with you?"

"No, Jessica and the children are home. I'm staying at the Metropole Hotel just up the street," he pointed. "I finished my last appointment just minutes ago."

"Why don't you join me for dinner?"

"No. You looked very into whatever you're reading. I hesitated even disturbing you."

"No problem." Catching the waitress' eye she looked at Kent. "What are you drinking?"

"Thank you. Iced tea is fine," he said, taking a seat.

Ann gave the order to the waitress, including a Blue Lagoon for herself.

They sat for two hours discussing books, politics, religion and law. Kent mentioned things about Danelaw influence on Anglo-Saxon jurisprudence that Ann hadn't been aware of.

"Enough of that," Ann finally said as she looked at the bay. "Isn't it a beautiful night?"

Kent was troubled. Even though she had impressed him as being a very mature and got-it-together person, her friendliness appeared unusual. Did she have any suspicions of him? "Do you have a big let-down after a case like Tabbetts? When did you arrive here?"

"Post-trial is a letdown. I drove to Corona del Mar State Beach, wandering around, trying to isolate myself from the world. Then to my boat. No radio on, nothing, got here yesterday evening."

Kent had followed her to the beach and marina. Everything matched.

"If you don't mind telling me," asked Kent, "what effect does the murder of Tabbetts have on you as a person and as his lawyer?"

"As his lawyer, I'm sorry to lose a client I think would have been acquitted. As a person, I don't know. The man was an enigma. Highly successful and full of quirks."

"You don't think he killed his son?"

Ann hesitated. "I don't think he did. Only an animal could kill like Robbie was killed, and Tabbetts wasn't an animal."

"Our higher base of social conduct differentiates us from animals, yet there are times when humans revert to animalistic behavior."

"Example?"

"Animals in a forest running from a fire. People in a theater piling up scores of dead at the doors while trying to escape a fire."

"I see your point, but do you equate that with a brutal murder?"

"I've merely illustrated we shouldn't be surprised when such things happen. You're very assured in the courtroom."

"We appear to be somewhat alike, unemotional and objective. I represent people who are usually at the bottom of the moral barrel. I don't kid myself about them, but they have a right to a defense." Ann paused and held his gaze. "Just as I think you would have that same right if you were criminally charged with someone's death."

Kent flinched and wondered if she were egging him on to reveal things he shouldn't. He liked her more and more, even though he was going to kill her. "Aren't you taking precautions about this killer?"

"Should I hide until he's caught? It isn't practical."

"But what about bodyguards or other measures?" Maybe she'd tell him something he didn't know.

She held his gaze. "Mr. Kent, this killer is intelligent and resourceful. If he wants to kill me he'll find a way to do it.

Frankly, I think he'll give me a sporting chance because," and she gave a broad smile, "I'm the weaker sex."

Kent wanted to smile.

Ann waved her hand. "Enough. It's not often I get to talk to a juror in circumstances like this. Critique some items for me?"

Kent smiled. "Me? Critique the great Ann Cavanaugh?"

Pleased by the compliment, Ann responded, "Don't worry, I'll evaluate it on my perceptions and experience." She hoped he'd become emotional about the trial and reveal traits similar to what Rush had experienced in telephone conversations with Hermes - if he were Hermes.

"On that basis, I accept." He smiled and finished his third glass of iced tea.

Kent tried to categorize and define his thoughts and feelings as Ann began her questions. Suddenly wary, and suspicious of her motives, he felt certain she must have her guard up. But, she'd have no more information than Rush had, no way of judging who is Hermes, but that might be the purpose of her conversation.

"What would your verdict have been based on the evidence you heard?"

"Guilty." He said it without rancor or admonishment.

She raised her eyebrows, obviously surprised by such a definite, unhesitant answer. "Really? Why?"

"Tabbetts should have grieved the loss of Robbie, whether or not he was his son. If Tabbetts had been traumatized by something in his past, his body language and or his face would show something unusual. Yet, when Lieutenant Briden confronted him, Tabbetts had his wits about him, became highly animated, communicative and demonstrated emotion. Those different characterizations didn't fit. Conclusion? Tabbetts didn't care about Robbie. He had no documentation of the family tragedy."

"That's it?"

"That's it. All that went before and after on that issue was just the law going through the motions of being ridiculous."

"Critique my performance."

Kent modulated his voice as though they were negotiating a business transaction. "Fine, but remember, you're the one who called it a *performance.*" A smile followed his friendly admonition. "You defended a child killer - a person you probably felt was guilty - and were doing all you could to get him acquitted. You allowed yourself to be used by the system to the same degree you were using the system." A mistake. His last sentence sounded like Hermes. Hopefully, standing alone, it wouldn't mean much to Ann.

Ann held his gaze and replied in a half-kidding tone. "You sound as though the whole criminal justice system is a joke."

"I don't respect it, if that's what you mean. But is my view much different from that of the public?"

He handled that nicely, she thought. Kent had never expressed that opinion or attitude when he was being questioned for the jury. It would have caused Rush and her to question him at greater length. She felt it best not to pursue that point.

His handsome profile bothered her. *Another clue?*

Ann laughed and held her hands up in the air. "Uncle! No more questions. Well, I better be turning in." She reached for the check, rejecting Kent's request to pay it.

"Thanks," Kent said as they shook hands. "It was an enjoyable evening. I should also get to bed. I'm going diving tomorrow."

"Me too. I'm sailing to Emerald Bay, near the other end of the island. It's beautiful, possibly dangerous. Would you like to join me?"

He appeared concerned about her privacy, "Won't I be interfering with your need to relax alone?"

"Not at all. I enjoy your company and I shouldn't be diving alone. Meet me at the dinghy area about six-thirty in the morning."

"Great! Look forward to it." They again shook hands.

KENT FELT UNEASY as he walked to the Metropole. He came here to kill Ann, knowing he'd have to be patient and choose an appropriate time and place. A gut feeling told him to get to know her, make the killing more sweet by knowing her motives, thoughts and secrets in defending the earth's scum. He laughed when he thought of it. It was like saying, "Hi, Ann, my name is Jonathan Kent and I'm going to kill you before the weekend is out. But first, let's talk, so I can know what makes people like you tick. See you later - at your moment of death." *Careful. I'm toying with her because she's a woman and not a real threat. That could lower my defenses.*

What would Ann think when, in the last moment of her life, she realized she had paid for Hermes' dinner and had actually invited him to go diving in an isolated area. Nothing would change his mind about killing her, but he had to admit she was very likable, well read, a good conversationalist and polite. Ann had none of the blustering or obnoxious egotism he had discerned in many lawyers.

The pleasant thought of killing Ann made him realize how much the deaths of the other lawyers and Tabbetts had washed away much of the anger of Phillip's death. He'd continue cleansing the system, and his own soul. The nightmares have practically disappeared. Anger had become a quiet resolve.

His uneasy feeling returned. The victim had invited him to go diving in a remote area. It was almost as if she had a death wish. That conclusion washed away by a thought that came out of nowhere. It didn't even seem like his. It were as though someone had knocked on his head, opened it and dropped in an alien message. It read: *What if Ann is actually setting this scene? What if she thinks you're the one with the death wish - that she intends to kill you?*

ANN SECURED THE DINGHY at the stern, undressed, and crawled into bed. It had been an interesting evening with Kent. It isn't often a person of that intelligence, education and maturity gets sworn in on a jury. He didn't mince words about Tabbetts' case. She didn't want to answer her next question. *Did I really come here to be found by Hermes so I could end* *being prey? I would end being prey if I could identify and kill him. But, what if he kills me?* Her practical side came out. *I shouldn't be diving alone.*

As she drifted off, she had one nagging thought playing at the fuzzy edges of her fatigue. A handsome, athletically-proportioned male juror - a Hermes' type figure - from the Tabbetts case, one day after the jury is dismissed, ends up in Avalon on business, goes to the far corner of the patio of a particular restaurant, at a particular time, just happens to meet the defense lawyer on the case, and had planned to go diving on Saturday morning. *Careful, think about this. There are too many coincidences. I need proof he's Hermes. By the time I get it I may be murdered.* She fell asleep.

"**TOWSON, DID YOU SEE** any identifying marks on Kent's face?

"Nah. Like wha'?"

"Any scars?"

"Nah."

"Did you notice anything below his left eye?"

"Nah, mostly seen da right side." Towson opened the door to his house and they entered.

Rush got information about where van Towson and his family could be located. "We expect a telephone call from you every day from the place you're staying and we'll call you back to verify. If you fail to do that just once we'll take you into custody and keep you there until the trial is over. Understood?"

Towson growled and nodded.

Walking to the RV, Rush dialed Ann's home and then her wireless phone number. The home message machine and her mobile phone were turned off. He left a message on her office machine. He telephoned the Irvine police station and got a return call from Hightower. Rush outlined the situation and added, "Get some people out to Ann's house. If she isn't there, find her. Have Anaheim police do the same with Judge Goldensmith." He looked at his watch. "It's one-thirty in the morning. We should be at my office by three. Call me with what you have."

Rush called two criminal prosecutors, two investigators, and Jane, his secretary. "We've identified Hermes. Meet at my office. Be prepared to stay until he's in custody." Disconnecting, he drummed his fingers and turned to Dunley. "Kent and I met and talked during *voir dire* on the Tabbetts' jury."

"He came across well."

"His hair is dark brown and crew cut, not the wavy long blond hair I imagined a Greek god would have. Then again, I sure as hell wasn't looking for Hermes to be one of the jurors."

"His hair is dyed, didn't you notice the blond hair on his arms?"

"No. I guess he did that so he wouldn't come across looking like a Greek god." Rush shook his head. "He must have been laughing every minute of the trial."

Dunley laughed. "One consolation. Ann would've never gotten an acquittal with Kent on the jury." He turned the radio on and off, an apparent nervous gesture. "Why is Ann still on Kent's priority list?"

"When Hermes called me at Tabbetts' house, I asked him when he was going to stop the killing. He answered that *some things are sacred.* I thought he meant his serial killing was a sacred thing, something ordained by the gods."

Dunley turned onto I-5. "This has to do with the UCLA expert's opinion?"

"Right. I didn't grasp the meaning of his statement. Hermes, as a Greek god, has a sacred number. It's four." Rush shook his head. "I guess his gods even put him in jury seat number four."

"Ann would be victim number six? How does that fit in?"

"We have five deaths so far but only four of them were lawyers. Kent called Tabbetts an appetizer, he doesn't count."

"So he kills in sets of four?" Dunley asked.

"That's what I think. Tabbetts was an interlude, a break. With his next lawyer victim he'll be on his second set of four with another interlude like killing a criminal defendant, judge, or a prosecutor. The criminal mind is sometimes precise, but it's always weird." Rush dialed the sheriff's office, told them he

147

needed to set up telephonic arrest and search warrants with the duty judge and that he would have the necessary affidavits ready within hours.

RUSH OUTLINED THE CASE to the personnel he had called into the office, the basic areas of inquiry, what specific information he was seeking and gave each of them an assignment. Dunley took charge of coordinating their efforts and keeping things flexible. "We need a paper trail of everything you do. If you need a drive-by, call the local police and request it ASAP."

When an hour had passed Rush stepped out of his office. "Let's see what we have."

An investigator spoke first, reading from notes. "Kent's residence is in Cowan Heights. Wife, Jessica, and three children under twelve. A son, Jeff, is the oldest. Kent's six feet one, one hundred and eighty pounds, blond wavy hair, blue eyes, forty-seven years old. He owns computer stores, the largest is located in Newport Beach. Very successful. No criminal record. Veteran, decorated, honorable discharge. He's also a reserve officer with Tustin PD, serving one weekend a month. Exemplary conduct and top-notch ability. He's a role model to veterans on the force."

"Reserve police officer! That explains a lot of things. A Newport Beach business?" Rush looked at Dunley. "When you checked out the victims on the Benedict case, did Kent's name pop up?"

"No, but I checked the list again since we got back and I saw a woman's name under a trust fund that's listed with the Kent address. First name, Jessica, is the same as his wife's. I assume it's a family inheritance under her maiden name to show as her separate property."

Rush looked around. "Dr. Ben, forensics, SWAT team?"

A deputy D.A. responded as he looked at his watch. "They should be ready about now."

"Anything on Ann?" He looked around.

Dunley replied. "No luck. If she's home she isn't picking up the phone. Her message machine is still off. Hightower said they've done everything to check her house except to break in. Her car isn't there. We got through to her office manager. Ann had called in two days ago - Thursday - and told her to cancel all appointments into next week. She didn't say what she'd be doing."

"What about the other residences?"

"No answer at her parents' vacation homes in Big Bear and Palm Springs. Police checked them out. What neighbors they found haven't seen her. Her parents haven't heard from her."

"About her boat," Rush said, "it's about a thirty-four footer, a Swan. The main sail has a replica of Lady Justice sewn into it in red. The stern slopes inward, which is not the usual sailboat profile. The name is *Crime Pays*. She's had it moored in Newport Bay for years."

"Not any more. The office manager said the boat has a new berth. Doesn't know where it is."

Rush grimaced. "Get back in touch with Ann's manager, have her go to the office and stay there. Fill her in on what we're doing and why. We'll need her as a front if Kent calls for any reason. Call the Irvine police and ask them to put an officer with her for the next twenty-four hours."

He turned to the group. "Thanks, very good work. Now get on the phones and contact every marina and mooring business in the county. Get people out of bed, get local police to knock on doors. Find out where Ann has her boat and get the names of the berth owners around hers. Is the boat still there? If not, contact the other owners to see if they've talked to her in the last three days about her plans. If there's nothing positive there, do the same for San Diego and Los Angeles Counties.

"Gentlemen, Jane, you've all worked with Ann when she was a prosecutor. Just two days ago Ann told me she didn't like being prey and she thought Hermes would probably make her acquaintance in some way and toy with her, because she's a girl, before he killed her."

Subdued laughter colored an investigator's response. "Kent expects to *toy* with Ann? I pity him."

The comment gave Rush strength. "I think she's intentionally disappeared because she wants to sucker him in without any interference from us."

"We'll find her, Rush, and she'll be fine." Heads nodded in affirmation.

EIGHTEEN

Saturday morning, seven o'clock. Streets meandered through an area of hillside homes on large lots. Dogs barked. A resident in pajamas and robe walked down his driveway for the morning paper.

Except for five vehicles in a caravan, moving as silently as possible through Cowan Heights, nothing indicated a quiet weekend would be disturbed. The sun, on the rim of the horizon, rose like an orange ball in the morning haze.

In sight of Kent's house, the caravan stopped. A helicopter appeared behind the house and took a stationary position above and to the rear of the backyard. Rush dialed his phone.

"Hello?"

He could hear children in the background. "Mrs. Kent?"

"Yes."

"Is Jonathan Kent home?"

"No. He won't be back until tomorrow."

"Do you know where I can reach him?"

"Who's calling please?"

"I need to get in touch with him. It's urgent."

"He's calling me from his next stop. I won't know where that is until some time this evening. Who's calling, please?"

"This is Rushton Jones, Orange County District Attorney's Office. I'm just outside your home with police units from Santa Ana, Tustin, Orange, and the Sheriff's office."

"Wh-what, what are you talking about."

"A sheriff's helicopter is at the rear of your home. I'm sure you hear it. We have a search warrant for your home, property and cars and an arrest warrant for your husband. For the safety of your family, I want you all to come out the front door immediately and walk to the street. You'll see the marked police vehicles."

"But - but - why...?"

Rush interrupted. "Are your three children in the house now?"

"Yes."

"Is anyone else in the house besides the children and you?"

151

"No. But - what's wrong? Why must we leave?"

"Mrs. Kent, I'll explain when you get out here. This is not a joke. Get out now with the children. When we come in we don't want kids suddenly popping out of a room or closet and being shot to death." A strong command. "Get them NOW! Come out here NOW!"

"Y-Y-Yes."

SWAT personnel darted out of two vehicles and took positions.

ANN MANEUVERED THE DINGHY to the dock and waved. "Good morning, glad you could make it."

Kent looked at the expanse of sky and water. "I wouldn't miss this for the world." He placed his spear gun in the dinghy, followed by his diving apparatus, and noticed Ann's fixation on the equipment.

"You own a rebreather?" She quickly turned away and looked out to sea, hoping she had hidden her fear.

"Yes," replied Kent. "Don't ask me why, but I got such a good sales talk I couldn't resist not owning one."

She headed for the boat as Kent settled into the dinghy. "The winds are tricky this time of year. We'll be tacking to Emerald Bay for about two hours."

"No problem. It's a perfect day."

"The water is clear, the reef is gorgeous and the Garibaldi are golden orange. It makes you feel like you're really above the water, floating around in space."

"Sounds great."

"Blue and mako sharks may be in the area but are not normally a problem. Shark's skin is too tough for our spears to do any realistic damage, the most it might do is frighten them off."

On the stern of the boat, the name stood out in bold letters: *Crime Pays.* Kent pointed to it. "Isn't that blatant?"

"No. People charged with crimes pay me to defend them. *Crime pays* me. *Crime Pays.* What could be more obvious?"

Kent's jaw appeared to tighten. His voice had a tinge of anger. "*Crime Pays* shouts out like an obscenity."

Ann didn't flinch. "Obscenity? Because I make money out of crime?"

"Yes, that, and advertising it as a boat's name."

"You're not being objective," Ann retorted. "Insurance companies are in legalized gambling, working the odds, because the law sanctions it. They have no risk until they accept the premium."

"But that's..."

"Would you object to an insurance company having a boat named *Gambling Pays*?"

"But..." Kent appeared more annoyed than exasperated.

Ann held up her hand. "Let me finish. Look at the commodity markets, options, derivatives, equity stocks. Legislation makes it legal. It's Las Vegas operating in New York and Chicago."

She waited, giving Kent time to respond. "It's not the same thing."

"Sure it is," Ann laughed.

Kent shook his head, apparently now knowing what to say.

"People are dying every day from the legal use of tobacco and alcoholic beverages. From farmers to corporations, people make a fortune out of the production and use of those drugs. Would you object to their boats being named *Drugs Pay*?"

Kent sighed. "You're a very intelligent and persuasive person. No wonder you turn juries your way."

Ann laughed and climbed out of the dinghy. "I agree with you, I'm one helluva woman and lawyer. Now, let's drop this dialogue and go see some fish."

Kent smiled. "I'm with you."

Kent heard waves washing against the hull as he looked at the jib and mainsail inhaling as much air as they could. It was a silence of sounds he keenly felt because it was natural to sailing. Yet, something about that silence bothered him. Something that would be an intrusion was missing; an unexpected silence.

"Ann, don't you want to turn on your radio? There may be some transmissions we should hear about weather or emergencies."

"No. When I'm out like this I don't want anything intruding on my privacy."

WHEN JESSICA KENT and the children reached the street, Rush identified himself and the police agencies, showed her the search warrant, gave her a copy, and told her they were about to enter the house to execute them.

"Again, is there anyone in the house?"

"No."

Jessica Kent appeared distressed, wanting explanations. Rush turned to Detective Mascotti. "Take them to safety. Fill her in."

The front door had been left open but SWAT members approached as though expecting heavy fire. They checked every room, the crawl space above the living quarters, the garage and the yard. No Jonathan Kent. The helicopter watch reported no one had left the house or appeared in the backyard since their arrival. An officer appeared at the front door and signaled forensics. "All clear."

Dr. Ben went by Rush. "Mrs. Kent said the workshop is in the garage. We'll search that first."

"Fine, I'll be with her if you need me." Rush climbed into the front passenger seat of a patrol car.

"Mrs. Kent, you're husband is stalking his sixth murder victim. We know who that is but can't find her. We must find him."

Covering her face with her hands, she sobbed. Rush motioned to Mascotti and she forcefully but smoothly pushed Mrs. Kent's shoulders up to an erect position, pulled her hands from her face and held them. "Mrs. Kent, help us before another person is murdered."

"I - don't - know - where - he - is." Her head drooped as she shook it. "I don't know. He's away on business."

"What about emergencies?"

"He has a wireless phone, pager."

154

"Do you have a phone in your handbag?"

Mrs. Kent nodded, opened her handbag and pulled it out.

"Call him. If he answers, try to learn exactly where he is."

She didn't move. Her head dropped again. "I can't...I can't...do that." The sobbing became heavy. "He's my husband. I love him." Looking up at Mascotti, she said, "I don't want anyone to die but I can't help without first speaking with him?"

Mascotti gently put a hand on her shoulder. "We understand. I'll talk to him." She took the phone. "What's his number?"

Mrs. Kent shook her head.

"Please, Mrs. Kent, if we're right, it means saving a life. If we're wrong, what harm can it do?"

She hung her head and mumbled the number.

Rush and Mascotti quickly discussed a plan for the few options they had. Mrs. Kent might unintentionally give everything away if she were to call. Mascotti dialed and waited for the ring.

"THAT'S YOURS," Ann told him, as she nodded toward his backpack, "I left my phone in my car."

If Ann were already suspicious of him it would only add to her unease if he let it ring. "Hello?" he said as he strolled to the bow, away from Ann.

"Hello! Mr. Kent?"

"Yes?"

Mascotti spoke hurriedly, with an excited tone. "My name is Mrs. LeGrand. I live in Cowan Heights. Your wife and children were in a bad accident. Some teenager came speeding over the hill at the curve and plowed broadside into your wife's van as she was leaving your driveway..."

"Are they OK?"

"Medics think she'll be fine. She gave me your number. The children were tossed around. They're all in ambulances as we speak. Where are you? How soon can you be here?"

Kent didn't respond.

"Mr. Kent, are you there."

The voice she heard was unreasonably calm and smooth. "Who are you? What kind of scam are you running?"

Mascotti motioned to Rush and shook her head as she said, "What? What? I don't understand."

Kent's voice remained calm, but it had a sharpness. "Bull. My wife and I have a secret code for telephone calls to make sure neither of us are talking under duress. She would have told you that."

Hurriedly, with annoyance, Mascotti replied, "My God, she's in no condition to start giving me a secret code, she…"

"Put Rush on the phone."

Mascotti turned pale. She handed the phone to Rush while shaking her head.

"Hello Hermes, or should I now call you Kent?"

"You keep disappointing me, Rush."

"Sorry. We're at your house with warrants. The game is up, why don't you tell us where you are and we'll come get you."

"Your concept of hunting is out of date. Let me speak to my wife."

Mrs. Kent's face was drawn and white. He had to take her hand and put the phone into it. He felt all their efforts to save Ann's life had fallen short.

"Jonathan, is it true? Have you murdered four lawyers and a defendant? Was that your alternative to counseling? Is that what's curing your nightmares?"

"Are you and the kids OK?"

"Jonathan! Jonathan!" she screamed, "answer me!"

"I love you. What I did, I did for my family and all the other innocent families out there, to protect you and all of them. You'll understand in time. Don't let the kids forget me. I was a loving father and a good husband. Let me talk to Rush again."

She dropped her hand to her lap and sat motionless. Rush picked up the phone.

"Rush here."

"Ann Cavanaugh is dead. Until I get to you, that'll cheer me up."

Rush didn't take the bait.   On the other hand, if he challenged Kent that Ann wasn't dead, it might make Kent hasten killing her if he were now able to do so. "Kent, in a short time we'll have you, dead or alive. We both want the criminal justice system to work better. Our methods differ. Tell me about it."

Kent didn't want to talk, but a tenuous rapport existed between them. Everything had come full circle.

"I had an older brother, Phillip. Our parents died when I was ten. Phillip was twenty-two. As a surrogate father, never marrying, he reared and guided me through an MBA at Stanford and gave me capital to start my business."

"You're fortunate to have had a brother like that."

"A robbery in Texas went awry. The suspects hijacked by brother's car." He detailed his brother's death, and added, "Defendants made no statements. No weapons found. It took three years before the first trial even started."

"My God, Kent, I'm really sorry..."

"The first conviction was reversed because of defense attorney incompetence. The second conviction because the defense claimed they hadn't received all the exonerating evidence from the prosecution. Jury instructions were prejudicial, and on and on..." Kent choked. "Almost thirteen years and the scums are coming up for their third trial. Witnesses can't be found. Others are now more reluctant to testify. Their memories have dulled."

"Kent, what can I possibly say?"

"Over all those years, do you know how many trips I made to Texas only to have court dates continued, motions unending, just waiting for them to get on with it?"

"Many people want to improve the system."

"I disagree. It appears easier to draw a paycheck from taxpayers and wear blinders. No accountability."

Rush bit his lip. How many times had he seen witnesses and victims humbled and worn down, so frustrated they wanted to drop criminal charges. "For what it's worth, Kent, I understand and appreciate what you're feeling. Sorry about your brother."

"That was the centerpiece of my decision to kill criminal defense attorneys." Kent then recited details about a churchwarden friend whose daughter had been kidnapped, raped and killed on her way home from an after-school job, his neighbor's wife who had been raped and murdered when she surprised a dope addict burglarizing her home, the Nathaniel Benedict case, and then cases he had read about in the newspaper. "The trials were *Opera Buffa.*"

"What you're doing isn't going to change the system."

"Maybe, but it has gotten wide publicity. And, rightly or wrongly, it has given me a great deal of satisfaction."

"Murder is never the solution, and you've done wrong by your family."

"Maybe one of you will start the ball rolling to correct the system's ills."

"Don't count on it. The current organization allows people to be anonymously lazy and unaccountable. By the way, I prosecuted the murderer of the warden's daughter."

"That's the reason I initially contacted you. You kept the court and defense attorney in line. I thought we'd see eye-to-eye."

Rush stepped out of the car and continued the conversation in private. "If you're taken alive, do you intend to plead not guilty and go to trial?"

"Yes. There's a thousand Baumholtzers and Polperros out there who'll drool over defending me."

"Like your brother's killers and all the lawyers and defendants you hate, do you intend to use the system?"

"Yes, that'll be stage two. The public will follow my trial. I'll give interviews and write essays about all the acceptably legal but absurd and often successful things being done to manipulate my case."

"You're forgetting one important aspect."

"Yes?"

"What your brother's killers inflicted on you, you're going to inflict on your family."

Silence.

"With your attorneys holding the hoops for the system to jump through, you'll still be on death row, with appeals pending, ten or twenty years from now, whatever."

"So?"

"Jeff will have gone from sixth grade through college and be married. He'll be living your agonies all those years, just like you lived with the aftermath of your brother's death."

"He'll have to shoulder that like I shouldered my brother's case."

"Multiply what I said by your two other children and your wife. Don't make them victims, don't add to their agony of losing a father and husband."

"If you take me alive, there's no alternative."

Softly. "You're wrong, Kent. There's an alternative."

"What's that?"

In a quietly even voice, Rush responded, "Kill yourself. Don't leave the years of trials and appeals as a legacy for your family."

No reply.

"Kent?"

"I heard you, Rush. It's nice to talk like civilized people, but I'll follow my convictions to the end, even if it means killing you."

DR. BEN raised an arm and gave a sweeping motion around the garage. "Here's corroboration. Literature on rebreathers, the copper bulb probably used on Baumholtzer," he pointed to the wall, "an extension cord with the wires exposed on one end. We also found fake moustaches and an assortment of hats and eyeglasses."

"Is the rebreather here?"

"No."

Rush turned to a Sheriff's sergeant. "That's it. I've got to leave. As soon as you're finished searching, let Mrs. Kent and the children back in. Here's the direct number to my office."

NINETEEN

"Business call," Kent finally offered. "My office thought it important." They had been sailing for half an hour and Ann hadn't asked him about the telephone call. Her lack of curiosity worried him.

Ann smiled. "I know how it is."

Kent wondered if Ann had received radio transmissions since Thursday with information she didn't want Kent to hear. Is that why she didn't have the radio on? Ann was too caring an individual not to want to be available if there was a nearby emergency. *Is she leading me into a trap?*

"EVERYBODY OUT HERE. I'll summarize the results," Dunley shouted as Rush entered. "Everything possible has been done in Palm Springs and Big Bear. Nothing. No car. The neighbors haven't seen or heard from Ann. We found her boat slip, it's in Dana Point. Empty. Authorities checked the boats in Avalon Bay. Ann's wasn't there. We got the boat's registration number. The police found her car in the marina parking area and are in the process of finding and checking with neighboring slip owners."

Rush's face sagged as he muttered, "God, I hope she isn't dead!"

The telephone rang. "Hello? Dunley speaking." He flipped the box switch as they gathered around.

"This is Lieutenant Hardy in Dana Point. We located a boat owner at the marina who had a conversation with Ann at the dock. She sailed to Catalina."

"When was that?"

"Last Thursday afternoon. There's something else."

"Yes?"

"A middle-aged male inquired about Ann's plans just after Ann sailed. The description of that person is a good match to your suspect, scar and all."

"Thanks." He hung up.

"All right," Rush said, "we have no choice but to concentrate on Catalina. Dunley and I will be going there as we try to find her location."

A prosecutor said, "The Los Angeles County Sheriff's Office on Catalina has no helicopters nor boats."

"What about trying to contact Ann?" Rush' impatience grew.

"The Coast Guard doesn't have any ships operating out of Catalina. Their nearest one is in Newport Bay. They and the Catalina office of the Los Angeles County Sheriff have been informed of the emergency. They're broadcasting over the regular channels and the emergency channel. If Ann is using herself as bait, she may not be listening. Either way, we're taking a chance. Kent could be hearing what she hears."

"What about a Los Angeles County Sheriff's helicopter on the mainland?"

"They usually have one in Long Beach, but it's miles away in Wrightwood and they can't release it. In any event, if they could, we'd be losing a lot of time waiting for it, refueling, and so forth. The Orange County Sheriff is agreeable to running their helicopter to Catalina and the Los Angeles Sheriff has no objection. They're picking up diving equipment."

Rush looked around. "Thanks, gentlemen, that's a damn good job."

He tried to inject some levity. "Ann's going to owe us one helluva big party on her boat, in Catalina."

Everyone cheered the thought as a tonic from the pressure of the morning.

"That's it then," Dunley said as he looked around the room. "You'll each have specific assignments now that we're focused on Catalina." He pointed to a prosecutor, "Contact the Sheriff's office. We'll be at their office in a couple of minutes. Fill them in on what we know. Notify the Los Angeles Sheriff in Catalina and the Coast Guard that we'll be on an Orange County Sheriff's helicopter and to use the secured line for all contacts with us. We want a description of Ann's boat and registration number broadcasted over the general channels and the emergency channel, asking boaters to respond if they've seen it."

161

Investigator Hardy broke in. "I just thought of something."

"Go ahead," said Rush.

"Helicopters are often hired by fishermen to fly off the Catalina shore looking for swordfish. We can try to communicate with them to keep an eye out for Ann's boat. It's better than depending on other boats."

"Do it! Kent knows he's been identified. The only saving grace we have is time. So long as he thinks Ann isn't aware of who he is - that she doesn't know he's Hermes - he'll figure he's somewhat safe to stick to his own schedule."

Dunley grabbed Rush as they headed for the door. "If one of us has to go into the water it should be me. Your connection to Ann may make you reckless."

"Kent knows me. If I confront him, there'll be a pause in his actions that may be critical for Ann and me."

"OK, but I don't like it. I'll get my Bowie knife from the RV. You may need the extra length in hand-to-hand combat."

Crossing the street, they went directly to the chopper pad on the roof of the Sheriff's forensics crime building. Deputy Marks waved. "Let's go."

THEY DROPPED ANCHOR in Emerald Bay. Sails were furled. No other boats in sight. Ann stretched and yawned. "Getting in the water will be a nice change of pace." Checking her diving equipment, she said, "I better hit the head."

As Ann went below, Kent turned off the speakers to below-deck, turned the radio to channel sixteen and put the volume just high enough to hear transmissions. Listening intently, he heard, "Ann Cavanaugh, aboard the *Crime Pays,* this is the Los Angeles Sheriff's Office in Avalon. Your office has an emergency. Please contact us and verify your receipt of this call."

Kent quietly and calmly replied. "This is *Crime Pays.* We got your message." He didn't break the connection. With his male voice responding on a call for Ann, he knew there might be questions. He'd divert them by carrying out a charade.

* * *

The Sheriff's dispatcher made an attempt to learn Ann's location without arousing suspicion. If someone was on the boat with her, it might be the killer.

"Would you please tell her to call her office ASAP? And please give me your position for my transmission log."

Kent felt the hairs climb on the back of his neck. *Law enforcement knows who I am, so they're trying to get a message to Ann to warn her.* Ann might come up in the middle of the conversation. It would be messy and not the constructive way he wanted to kill her. "We're on our way to San Diego, about three hours out of Avalon." He signed off and turned off the radio.

His mind hurdled through the possibilities. *How long have they been trying to reach Ann? Is she stalking me? Did Ann hear the broadcast since she left for Catalina and now she doesn't want me to hear it?* He dismissed that possibility. *If the authorities had been searching for Ann they would have checked the boats in Avalon Bay and found her before we left.* He concluded the broadcasts must have begun this morning, since they left the harbor. *It's consistent with the ruse Rush tried to pull when they called me. So what about Ann? Does she really have the nerve or strength to take me on alone? Would the cops put Ann in that position?*

His mind quickly came to another hurdle. *What's the purpose in warning Ann? She already knows Hermes is targeting her. Of course, they want to tell her Hermes is Jonathan Kent.*

How did they identify me? I had no connection with any of the victims. Fingerprints? Shoe prints? Nothing. How then? The rebreather? Is that why Ann asked about my rebreather?"

Was her trip to Catalina just to lure me into a trap, Ann vs. Hermes? Could she be that cocky and confident?

Ann came on deck. Her eyes fixed on his right hand. He hadn't replaced the mike. Nonchalantly, he placed it on the console.

"Were you making a transmission?"

163

"No. I was just standing here, looking over the console. I guess I unconsciously picked up the mike."

Her reply was friendly but insistent. "Jonathan, would you like to make a call? Here, I'll get it set up for you." She took the microphone and handed it to Kent.

Kent replaced it on the console. "No, but thanks anyway. I have my phone if I need to call anyone. I'll go to the head and then we can see those Garibaldi."

He stepped around her and went below, making sufficient noise so Ann would know his location. Quickly, he returned to the hatch leading to the deck, listening to determine if Ann had turned on the radio. *My imagination is flying too high. I'm giving her too much credit for guts.* Kent returned to the head, flushed, opened and closed the door with a bang and went back on deck.

As he came into view, Ann asked, "Jonathan, that's a helluva large barb on the end of this spear. Where did you find that?"

"I made it."

Ann ran her thumb over the barb, shook her head and put the spear back on deck.

THE PILOT'S VOICE sounded ominous as Rush finished putting on his diving gear. "A male person purportedly on Ann's boat answered the Sheriff in Avalon, advised them they had received the emergency message and were on their way to San Diego, three hours out of Avalon. He was asked to have Ann call her office ASAP."

"Anything else?" asked Rush.

"Yes. The Sheriff said the person on the boat seemed quietly abrupt and showed no interest in inquiring about the type of emergency or anything else."

"How soon will we be in Avalon?"

The pilot pointed out the port side. "We should be landing in two minutes."

Rush looked at his watch. "Maybe we should fly toward San Diego?"

At about five hundred feet, the blade pitch and noise changed as the helicopter rapidly angled toward Emerald Bay.

"Sheriff is on the line again. A swordfish helicopter spotted Ann's boat in Emerald Bay, verifying the name with binoculars. They didn't fly low or do anything that might attract the boat's attention and they immediately left the scene."

"Did they see anyone on the boat?"

"Affirmative. They saw two people in diving gear."

"It has to be Ann and Kent." murmured Rush.

TWENTY

The brief appearance of the helicopter bothered Kent. He couldn't see identification markings. It appeared too small to be a government helicopter. *But wouldn't police be using a small chopper to not arouse my suspicions?*

He had planned on killing Ann at his leisure, with specific plans for the body and the boat. Now, just killing her was the sole priority.

Each had a spear gun with a four-foot spear as they descended to thirty feet, ten feet apart. The accurate and lethal effectiveness of a band spear gun is about three times the length of the spear. Ann pointed to the reefs and the Garibaldi. Kent thought, what a beautiful place for Ann to die.

Kent's peripheral vision saw Ann make a sudden and unexpected move. Quickly turning his head, he saw her leveling her gun toward him and shooting. His adrenalin surged. *She knows I'm Hermes! But she wouldn't kill me in cold blood!* That thought was eliminated by what he was seeing. *My God, she set me up for this! All this time I've been stalking her and I've been her prey!*

THE SHERIFF'S HELICOPTER hovered almost at water level just off the starboard of *Crime Pays.* Rush sat on the edge of the open hatch. With one motion, he swung himself to the landing gear and slipped into the water.

KENT WHIRLED toward Ann while bringing up his gun. Her spear went by his head. The gun ripped from her hands as he shot his large-barbed spear.

The cord attached to Ann's spear cut sharply against his face. The gun followed, striking him a hard blow and tearing into his flesh as it whipped against his head and face. Blood stained the water. Despite the pain, he turned to follow Ann's gun and saw a shark swimming away, with her spear embedded in its mouth and the gun dangling behind. *Ann saved my life!?*

Various emotions ran through his mind and body. Objectivity returned.

Kent's spear struck Ann's left thigh. The large barb made it impractical to pull out. Blood flowed and she thought of the sharks. Only one reasonable conclusion existed. Kent was Hermes. If Kent had been an innocent diver not intent on killing her, his normal reaction would have been confusion and hesitation when he saw her fire in his direction. That would have given him enough time to see her gun being carried away by the shark. Only Hermes would have reacted as Kent did.

Holding onto the spear and stabilizing it made her more comfortable with the pain. She fought the mental trauma and physical shock, knowing Hermes would be coming in for the kill. Kent would have to conclude he had given himself away.

The tug on her hand confirmed her thoughts. Kent pulled on the cord with a side-to-side motion, attempting to mutilate her leg and cause more pain. Ann tried to move her body and the cord in her hand in unison with Kent's movements to keep the spear from gouging the inside of her thigh. She reached for her knife to cut the cord from the spear, but found an empty sheath. With all the talk on board about radio transmissions and Kent's large-barbed spear, she had forgotten her knife.

He'll pull me toward him, grab the end of the spear and work it around the inside of my thigh as he playfully uses his knife on the rest of my body. I'll be like a piece of meat on a stick.

Kent saw Ann reach for her knife and reveled in what she had to be thinking when she found it missing. He had covered it while they were on deck, taking the chance she wouldn't do a final check. He'd now kill her in a slow and painful manner. Knowing she was going to die, she'd do whatever she had to do to kill him. He'd pull her close enough to wiggle the spear inside her thigh and yet hold her far enough away so she couldn't grab him or his air hose. His knife would do the rest. He pulled on the cord, just as another diver, with knife drawn, came into his vision.

167

* * *

With minimum movement of her head, she tried to keep Kent within her vision as she tried to learn why he had looked upward. *It may be a trick.* She saw a diver coming directly toward her. *Kent has an accomplice? I'm dead.*

Kent watched the diver going to Ann. If they were together he couldn't attack both and survive. He'd have to immediately immobilize or kill Ann. Dropping his gun, and while Ann appeared distracted by the third diver, he darted forward. As he kicked swiftly past Ann to lessen any possibility of being grabbed, he slashed at her with his knife.

Ann turned in time to see Kent coming. One hand tried to keep the spear in her thigh from moving from the weight of the gun dangling in the water. She kicked away and, with her other arm, slightly deflected the knife, but not quickly enough. The knife cut her wet suit at her breasts and sliced into her air tube. Adjusting her position, looking at Kent, she waited for another attack. Kent swam fifteen feet beyond her and looked at the third diver.

Keeping Kent within her view, Ann again glanced at the third diver, turned, and prepared to fight them both. The third diver made a circle with the index finger and thumb of the left hand and stuck the right index finger through it. It was the signal Rush and she used when, as prosecutors, they had screwed over a defendant on cross examination. Rush, keeping an eye on Kent, swiftly kicked to Ann and cut the spear cord.

The presence of a diver going to Ann's aid appeared to put Kent in limbo. Rush motioned her to the surface. Her presence would be a hindrance in any battle with Kent, and, more blood would attract sharks.

Her partially-cut air tube had a safety valve that reduced the opening of the escaping air, but still prevented water from entering the breathing apparatus. She tested the amount of air. It appeared adequate, but caution was essential. Taking a slow deep breath, she noted her depth was thirty feet. At a rate of one foot per second she slowly expelled air.

Rush positioned himself between Ann and Kent. When he felt Ann was safe, Rush extended his left arm, indicating to Kent to surface and surrender.

Kent extended his middle finger.

Rush controlled his anger but was glad Kent wasn't surrendering. Killing him will save years of diarrhea justice, spinning the law and the facts, the media circus and all the attendant freakish things. His family would be spared many things. He felt relieved he'd be killing Kent, even though he also might die.

Firmly grasping the Bowie knife he watched Kent maneuver closer.

As the distance narrowed to six feet, they did an underwater ballet, trying to gain advantage for a knife thrust. Whoever inflicted the most damage on the first thrust would be able to kill the other at his leisure. *Even if I'm not ready, I'll have to strike when he does. I won't get another chance. It'll be over in seconds.*

He circled around Kent, maneuvering him to the approximate area where Ann had been bleeding. The blood from Hermes' face added to the discoloration of the water. Rush held up the plug nickel Kent had sent to Ann, and dropped it, pointing, indicating Kent would soon be on the ocean floor.

Kent smiled, feeling secure he would kill Rush as he hoped Ann would probably die from the wound he had inflicted. He closed the gap between them, switching his knife from hand to hand, and suddenly making a feint with his left hand.

Rush saw the knife in Kent's right hand and didn't fall for the feint. He defensively threw up his left hand to ward off the expected thrust. Kent's knife hand came forward in a swift but wide-arc. Rush reacted like a batter who saw a curve ball breaking to his stomach. Maintaining the position of his shoulders and feet, he pulled back the middle part of his torso, shaping his body into a V. Kent's knife slashed through the water where Rush's abdomen had been, going upward, slicing into his face and ear, as Rush thrust the Bowie into Kent's abdomen.

When Kent's knife arm completed its upward arc, Rush grabbed it with his left hand as he repeatedly shot the Bowie into Kent, slicing and twisting with each thrust.

Kent's blood clouded the water. Resistance stopped. Rush saw an arrow-like figure. Then another. Facing them, he backed off as he pressed his left forearm and hand against his face and ear, keeping the escaping blood to a minimum.

Ascending slowly from thirty-five feet, he saw more sharks arriving. They hit Kent like competing athletes, twisting and turning for their share of the reward.

Kent, turning in agony, saw the sharks. Without hesitation, he pulled out his mouthpiece and exhaled, deciding drowning was the quicker and better alternative. As water filled his lungs, last thoughts flitted through his mind. *This is the way Franco Polperro must have felt when I pulled him under.* And, not losing his sense of the grotesque, *I'm dying in a sea of lawyers.* He felt the multiple jolts as his body whirled through the water, being dismembered.

DUNLEY AND THE CO-PILOT pulled Rush aboard and placed him on deck next to Ann. She was on her back, immobilized .

He had just killed someone. The rationalization was that he had defended himself against an attack by a murderer - a person who had killed five people and was trying to kill Ann when he entered the scene. On the other hand, he could have just followed Ann to the surface, covered the area with law enforcement personnel, and waited for Kent to surface. The liberals are going to have a field day with that argument. *No! The only sure way was to end it as I did. No regrets.* Though he would never admit it to anyone, he felt he had saved Kent's family years of anguish. *Let them get on with their lives.*

The helicopter hung in the air a hundred feet off starboard. Dunley and the co-pilot finished attending to Ann. They had cut away the wet suit at the thigh, medicated the area where the spear had entered, packed it with bandages to control the bleeding, splinted the leg and taped the spear to the splints to immobilize it and the leg.

"Dunley and I can get Ann on the helicopter. Then you. Hospital emergency has been alerted. We'll have you both there in minutes." The co-pilot reached toward Rush's wounds.

Rush pulled away. He spoke with a tired but pointed voice. "No! Tend to Ann, save her life so I can beat the hell out of her when she recovers."

Ann gave what sounded like a painful laugh. Ignoring Rush's statement, the co-pilot cut the hood away from the wound.

Her eyes opened as she wearily managed to whisper, "I catch a serial killer for you and all I hear is bitch! bitch! bitch!"

"It's a long slash, not a stab wound. Kent took quite a nick out of your ear," Dunley concluded.

Rush laughed through the pain as a feeling of disorientation came over him. He couldn't remember when he had last had a full night's sleep. Looking at Ann he managed a smile. "You were lucky. If those sharks had arrived any sooner they could have hit you first."

"They wouldn't touch me." She was breathing heavily and grimacing. "Professional courtesy." A low coughing laughter followed. "Did he get away? Do I have to do it over again? God! I can't get good help nowadays."

Slightly wheezing and with a strained tone, he replied, "It's over. Two of our brethren finished with a final verdict. No appeals."

She grimaced again and raised her eyebrows. "Tell me what happened."

The co-pilot waved the helicopter in for evacuation.

Rush didn't respond. Moments passed. Ann stopped Dunley from preparing her to board the helicopter. She asked again, "What happened?"

Rush closed his eyes, swallowed hard and waited for his throat to relax. In a voice Ann strained to hear, he said, "Hermes is dead." Opening his eyes, he managed a teasing half-smile. "You *Rushed In* - put our lives in jeopardy. I saved yours. We're even. I hope you're mature enough to handle that. I don't want to have to kick you out of my home six months from now."

Ann struggled through her sedation and squeezed Rush's hand.

THE END